Clara's Choice

J. Willis Sanders

BUGGS ISLAND BOOKS

Printed in the United States of America
Cover art by BookCoverZone.com

By J. Willis Sanders
Learn more about these books at
https://jwillissanders.wixsite.com/writer

The Eliza Gray Series
The Colors of Eliza Gray
The Colors of Denver Andrews
The Colors of Tess Gray

The Forgiveness Quilt: An Amish Christmas Carol
The Easter Prayer: An Amish Easter Story

The Clara Engelman Series
Clara's Mourning
Clara's Courtship
Clara's Choice

The Essence of Emmaline Strong

The Outer Banks of North Carolina Series
The Diary of Carlo Cipriani
If the Sunrise Forgets Tomorrow
Love, Jake

The Hope Series
The Coincidence of Hope
The Yearning of Hope
The Gift of Hope

Writing as J. D. James
Reid Stone: Hard as Stone
Reid Stone: Red Rage

Reviews for The Colors of Eliza Gray
https://www.amazon.com/dp/B092RKPZBM

"Captivating! … J. Willis Sanders has captured love in this story. Love of a father to his daughter, love between brothers and sisters, and true love struggling to find a way to a future together. I look forward to Sanders' next book."

"I can honestly say that "The Colors of Eliza Gray" had me hooked from chapter one! It had me wishing for a "happily ever after" for Eliza from the beginning. Every emotion is found in this book and J. Willis Sanders definitely knows how to draw his readers in! I had read half of it before I realized it and finished it up the next morning!"

"Enjoyed this book so much! Stayed up way past my bedtime to finish it. Romantic and inspiring story. Great descriptions enabling the reader to visualize the scenes. Highly recommended."

"You won't be able to put this awesome book down! Love, love of a father and their love!!!! Please write another about how their lives are going!!!"

"The Colors of Eliza Gray is one of the most compelling books I've ever read. Beginning with a hearing-impaired abused Eliza. Taking you through her education and life altering experiences once she has her world opened to her. I truly hated it to end."

Reviews for The Christmas Quilt:
An Amish Christmas Carol
https://www.amazon.com/gp/product/B0BNVQDKD1

"The Forgiveness Quilt is a wonderful book that can be read in one sitting or chapter by chapter. I took it with me on a long journey, and it made the trip so much more enjoyable. The book is well written and engaging throughout, with great descriptions of the setting as well as the characters. I highly recommend this as a pre-Christmas read!"

"This is the first book I have read by J. Willis Sanders but will not be the last. A very uplifting and inspiring book."

"In The Forgiveness Quilt, Sanders set a substantial challenge for himself: to recreate Charles Dickens' journey of writing A Christmas Carol in just six weeks. As a writer myself, I understand how challenging it can be to write just the first draft of story of this length in six weeks, let alone completing all the work necessary for refining the draft and preparing it for publication. With compelling characters, the sad journey of a heart hardening over time, immune to messages of love and joy, and its final, almost too late redemption, Sanders has succeeded in his challenge and created a moving holiday story of hope and redemption."

Reviews for The Outer Banks of North Carolina Series
https://www.amazon.com/gp/product/B098P67LJB

The Diary of Carlo Cipriani

"This is fascinating tale of survival, both of shipwrecked sailors and of how wild horses came to live on the Outer Banks. I enjoyed the characters and the character development, as well."

"The heartfelt descriptions of the characters brings them to life and bids you to follow their stories. There is life and love, despair and grief that eventually give way to hope for the future. A well written, intriguing story that bids me to learn more about the Outer Banks."

"Many twists and turns, lots of tragedy but always hope. At several points you are not sure what is real and what is the narrators madness due to his loneliness. A very satisfying resolution answers all our questions."

If the Sunrise Forgets Tomorrow

"What a captivating book. I read it in 2 sittings because we just couldn't put it down. Brought tears to my eyes!"

"This book was captivating and it was difficult for me to put it down. If you like a touch of history and have a love for Ocracoke, this is a great book to read. It was very descriptive and made me feel like I was there. Virginia and Ruby are typical sisters who are loving each other one minute and the next they are disagreeing. I enjoyed the strength they displayed as they overcame many obstacles. A Great Read!"

"To be honest, I wasn't certain I would enjoy this book. I've read other books at in the Outer Banks and a lot of them seem to be sloppily written and just capitalizing on the setting to prey on die-hard OBX readers. I was pleasantly surprised to find it very well written and descriptive. It was easy to visualize the island, the characters, and the story as it all unfolded. I would recommend checking it out!"

Reviews for The Coincidence of Hope
https://www.amazon.com/gp/product/B0B2KZ9KPM

"This is not war story, nor an action novel. It's not a love story. No, it's more than that, as it touches on many love stories, life stories, and stories of hope, as glimpsed through the thoughts of Joe's ghost. Excellent characterization, clever points of view. Revelations throughout the telling will surprise you. The story of hope that Sanders has created will grab you and keep you engrossed until the very end."

"Trust me when I saw you won't need a tissue but a whole box, this storyline really tugs at your heart and you won't be the same after reading it. I'm really looking forward to see where book 2 will take me. Give this book a change it's so very worth your time."

Dear readers,

The main character in this book is a young Beachy Amish Mennonite woman. There are many different Amish orders. One reason I chose this order is because they can use any technology except radios and television, which can lead to some interesting plot devices such as using cell phones and driving vehicles. A quick internet search of the Beachy Amish Mennonites shows why they don't use TV or radios, as well as the general rules they follow, also known as their Ordnung, which can vary greatly from community to community like with most Amish Ordnungs. Interestingly, according to research, they also don't speak Pennsylvania Dutch like most Amish do.

Although this book is fiction, I tried to write it accurately by researching it online and asking questions on online forums. Yes, all Amish value faith, family, and community, but I think we can be sure that life's challenges, just like anyone else's challenges, can cause turmoil in their lives.

The Amish and Mennonites are interesting people with admirable work ethics and dedication to God, and I enjoy writing about them in such a way as to make them have human frailties like the rest of us. After all, a good story includes conflicts like we all have. Since many of those conflicts happen when we search for someone to love, it's likely the Amish and Mennonites may experience the same thing depending on the individual and the circumstances, which is where the magic of fiction takes over. Yes, I'm smiling, because I dearly love the magic of fiction.

Also, if you've read my Eliza Gray series, you'll recognize some of the side characters in this book from that series. No doubt some readers of the series would like to get glimpses of their lives after the series ended, so this is why I chose to include them, as well as my hometown of Clarksville, Virginia, and the surrounding counties of Charlotte and Halifax and the town of South Boston.

If you'd like to visit a great website about the Beachy Amish Mennonites, here's the link: http://www.beachyam.org/

If you'd like to visit Clarksville online to learn about it and Kerr Lake, what us locals call Buggs Island Lake, visit https://clarksvilleva.com/#/

Thank you for reading,
J. Willis Sanders

Clara's Choice

Chapter 1

Standing at the podium, Samuel faced the community members gathered around the living room and kitchen. "Welcome to our Sunday service. I'd like to start with a verse to remind us of the beauty of spring, which just came yesterday according to the calendar." He opened his Bible. "Isaiah 55:12. 'For ye shall go out with joy, and be led forth with peace: the mountains and the hills shall break forth before you into singing, and all the trees of the field shall clap their hands.' Let us pray."

Clara closed her eyes. She was sitting with John and Edna on one of the benches at the kitchen table. Beside John sat Noah, now a member of the community, having joined three months after

Vernon left last year in October. The news had both shocked and pleased Clara's parents. Both had hoped Noah would court and marry Clara and bring her home to be near them, but they were happy to hear that Vernon had seen the light, so to speak, with how he and Clara weren't a good match, which was what Clara had told them. As always, she regretted lying, but she had promised to keep Vernon's lies about his wife a secret. His story of her mental illness and how it had affected his life deserved forgiveness. God, of course, had already forgiven Clara's sin of lying, for he knew her heart and why she had done so. Vernon had suffered enough. He had seen the error of his ways and should be allowed to serve God in another community.

Samuel finished his prayer and raised his head. "It's good to have Jonah, Lydia, and Tess join us today. As we have decided by vote when they asked about coming, we won't turn away anyone from hearing God's word whether they are English or Amish. Now, the message today will also come from Isaiah 55:12."

As Samuel continued, Clara could hear the soft breaths of Jonah, Lydia, and Tess on the bench behind her. Although Jonah and Lydia had come to the Sunday service once a month since October, this was Tess's first visit since he had started taking guitar lessons from her last September. According to Alison, Lydia said the lessons now included regular visits to Tess's home. So far, though, the visits seemed innocent enough, spent fishing from her dock or going out to supper in Clarksville, but the chance of romance with her must've been on Jonah's mind.

To Clara's left, John fidgeted. Patting his knee, Noah caught her eye and winked. His delay in asking to court her was a surprise. Not only had he saved her from a marriage with Vernon, he was now renting Vernon's home north of Nathalie. Acting more like a big brother than a potential beau, he visited Clara and the children once a week or so, saying he wanted to make sure they didn't need anything done around the house. Although his delay in asking to court her was a surprise, she attributed it to his understanding of how she needed time to get over the blow of Vernon lying to her.

From behind Clara, the faint aroma of perfume came from Tess. Lydia had never worn it that Clara had noticed, odd for English women. Perhaps Tess wore it for Jonah, trying to attract him like a bee to a flower. As much time as they spent together, he was more like a spider caught in her web.

Clara knew she shouldn't but she envied Tess's full figure. Compared to her, Clara looked like a skinny scarecrow. No wonder Jonah was attracted to her. At least she was wearing a blue, knee-length skirt and a white sweater with a neckline well above her cleavage to the service. If not, Samuel might not be able to keep his eyes averted, especially from her lustrous auburn hair flowing over her shoulders and down her back. Yes, Jonah must be smitten, so how long before he proposed to her?

Taking in a labored breath, Clara hated the thought of Jonah married. Since she had realized she loved him—no, she was *in* love with him—her days and nights had been spent trying to purge him from her mind. Noah's visits helped, but always, whether gathering eggs, milking the cow, or doing any other farm chore, that night in Pennsylvania, when they had gone on a drive, haunted her with his living presence. He must've sensed her unease about courting Vernon, or he wouldn't have called her from his hotel room to start with. Then, when they had parked by a river and she had brazenly crawled into his lap with her hair down like a child to be comforted, she had felt nothing like a child. Those few moments had been intimate but not. Although he held her close, it was the embrace of a friend when she'd rather he embrace her as a man.

That night was gone and never would return. It was time to look past Jonah and consider Noah as a husband, plus the father John and Edna needed.

Clara caught snippets of Samuel's sermon, thoughts of Jonah and Tess as distracting as an annoying fly. Behind her, Tess whispered something to Jonah and he whispered back. Words of love? A proposal at this very moment?

Samuel closed the Bible. "I hope no one minds if my sermon isn't as long as it should be. I'm still trying to get the hang of preaching. Let's stand and sing *How Great Thou Art*. Then we'll have the blessing and enjoy this fine meal the ladies prepared.

Everyone stood and sang. Jonah and Tess, no doubt, preferred to play guitar to accompany the voices, but that was never voted on in this congregation. Behind Clara, their rich voices joined as one, aggravating Clara even more. *Really*, she thought, *like the English say, you two should get a room.*

The song ended. Samuel said the blessing. At the table, the ladies uncovered bowls and platters, releasing the aromas of chicken, beef, and pork, either in individual dishes or in casseroles with gravy oozing around the sides. A line formed.

Plates were filled with green beans, boiled potatoes, beets, buttered rolls, and slices of meat. Eyes darted at vanilla crumb pie, apple fritter bread, and sugar cookies, all waiting to be served for dessert.

Clara filled the children's plates. They went outside to join Alison's boys, who were sitting with their plates in their laps and their feet dangling off the porch. Noah was standing in a corner with Samuel. They alternated between talking and eating from the plates they held in one hand, a fork in the other. Lydia, Alison, and Tess were huddled in a corner of the kitchen, their plates on a counter. The rest of the small community sat in chairs, chatting between bites and sips of lemonade.

Tess joined Clara at the table and filled a glass with lemonade. "Alison sure loves to gossip. Before Lydia came over, she wanted to know if Jonah and I were dating."

Clara wanted to know that very thing herself. "Well, I wouldn't call it gossip if there's truth in it."

Tess sipped lemonade. Jonah had walked over to Samuel and Noah. His huge smile suggested he was talking about playing the guitar.

"I don't understand why some lucky girl hasn't snagged Jonah yet?" Tess turned from him to face Clara. "Do you?"

Sipping lemonade, Clara lowered the glass. "I was hoping you could tell me why, as much time as you spend with him."

Tess's full lips, shaded with pink lipstick, fought with what resembled a smile and a frown. "I'm not the one watching him so intently. I understand he's been a great help to you around the farm. He's told me a lot about you and he and Lydia and your children since we met during your camping trip at Occoneechee State Park. It's Clara this and Clara that, John this and Edna that. To hear him talk, he would like to be their dad."

Clara clenched her teeth. No doubt Tess would rather have him be a dad to *her* children. "What's Denver doing while you're here?" Clara's character didn't let her say the rest: *I understand you and Eliza trade him on weekends.*

"They're home from church by now. We attend a country church not too far outside of Clarksville."

Lydia came over. "Well, ladies, what do you think of these handsome Amish farmhands?" She nodded toward the corner with Jonah, Samuel, and Noah. "Especially Noah. If I tried, I bet I could make him leave your little community to marry me."

Drinking lemonade again, Clara swallowed before she strangled herself. The audacity of such a statement was beyond belief.

Tess laughed. "He's handsome all right, but my Jonah has them *all* beat." She looked at Clara. "Don't you think so?"

Carrying a slice of vanilla crumb pie, Alison hurried over. "I heard that. I know I'm supposed to say my Samuel is the handsomest man here, but I could eat Jonah up like this pie."

More audacity, and from Clara's best friend at that. Rather than shame her friend, Clara left for the porch. The screen door squeaked behind her, followed by another squeak. "I saw you talking to Tess," Jonah said. "She's something else, isn't she?"

"She sure is, for a woman who trades her sister's husband every other weekend."

Jonah laughed. "You and your jokes. Besides, you know better than that. She explained their situation when we met them on our camping trip in the park." He stepped around in front of her and looked her in the eye. "Enough of that. I keep expecting to hear about you courting Noah."

Clara took a step backward. "I keep expecting to hear you're going to marry Tess, as much time as you spend with her."

Jonah grinned. "Well, the idea is tempting. I love her Dutch accent from when she and her family were Amish in Ohio. Eliza's story is amazing, falling in love with Denver when he was her sign language teacher and becoming a famous artist. That's as romantic as romantic gets."

With hot tears welling at her confused feelings, Clara whirled around and faked a sneeze. "I think I'm catching a cold," she said, taking a handkerchief from her pocket.

The screen door squeaked open. "A cold?" Noah asked.

"Maybe," she said. "I should get the children in the pickup and get home before I spread it around."

"Your nose isn't even stuffy," Jonah said.

Noah tilted his head to one side. "If she said she has a cold, Jonah, she has a cold. I'll get your dishes and put them in the truck, Clara. Jonah, maybe you can be nice enough to get the children in the truck."

As Noah went inside, Jonah looked into Clara's eyes again. "I apologize, Clara, if you are sick." He paused. "I was only teasing about Noah. I'm not sure if he can make you as happy as Abram did. I hope you know all I want is for you to be happy."

Nodding, Clara ducked her head. "I know. Thank you." A sudden thought raised her eyes to his. "You never wired the rest of the house last fall. Do you think you can before the summer heat gets here? Air conditioning sounds wonderful."

"Yeah. My herd coming down with Foot Rot had

me as busy as I could be. Thank the Lord they're doing okay now."

Carrying two covered plates, Noah opened the screen door. "I'll get this and the children in the truck. I see your neighbor isn't going to do it."

Jonah eyed him as he strode toward John and Edna, kicking a ball with Alison's boys. Clara touched his sleeve. "I'm sorry I was short with you. Do you know how we get in bad moods sometimes and don't know why?"

"I do exactly. I'll stop by tomorrow and look over the house again. I need to make a list of all the supplies we need. Right now I'll try a slice of that vanilla crumb pie."

"See you tomorrow." Clara watched him go inside. At the pickup, Noah waved her over and opened the door for her.

After she climbed in, he shut the door and leaned his elbows on the window opening. "I'm going to drive to Pennsylvania this week after I plant my garden and see my folks." He tipped his wide-brimmed straw hat back, revealing blond hair and blue eyes.

For Clara, those features didn't hold the same charm they had when they were teenagers. "Have a safe trip. If you see my folks, tell them I hope to visit soon."

Noah said he would and left for his pickup, which he had traded his car for not long after he rented Vernon's house. It seemed he was putting roots down in southern Virginia for good. Considering his and Clara's past, she knew why.

Now to get home and plan the planting of her own garden. Not wanting to go back inside, she made a mental note to call Alison tonight and apologize for leaving without saying goodbye.

She just didn't feel like facing Tess again.

Chapter 2

The next morning, when Clara returned home after taking Edna to school at Alison's house, she found Jonah's pickup truck parked in her driveway, him sitting on the tailgate and swinging his feet like a boy. He waved and smiled as she neared him. Despite trying to purge her feelings for him from her heart, she couldn't help waving and smiling too.

She parked between his pickup and the house, and he opened her door. "Don't you look fresh as a daisy this morning, Clara. I think spring agrees with you."

Taking a huge breath, Clara agreed. Crisp and clean, the air refreshed her. "I do love spring." Eyeing him, she tilted her head to one side. "You seem quite happy this morning."

"I am, I am. Tess invited me to supper last night. After we ate, we went to her dock and fished for catfish. Lydia doesn't really like fishing, so she stayed at home."

Clara was tempted to frown. A romantic moon, full and glowing, had risen last night. No doubt it had illuminated the lake for fishing—and possibly kissing and hugging. Then again, maybe Tess's two children had stopped that from happening. She looked up at Jonah. "Do Tess's children like to fish?"

"Very much, but they were with Denver and Eliza."

Of course they were, Clara thought. *So you and Tess could be alone and do things you shouldn't do, since you're not married.*

"After we cleaned the fish," Jonah added, "we played our guitars and sang. Tess invited me to her church to sing and play with her. I'm really looking forward to it."

Behind Clara, her truck door slammed, and she whirled around. Caught up in thoughts of Jonah, she had left John in the truck. He pattered toward her and Jonah, his leather shoes scattering gravel. "Mama! You forgotted me!"

Jonah chuckled. "Hey there, John."

Clara knelt beside him. "I'm sorry, sweetheart."

She stood to face Jonah. "I know I should correct his 'forgotted,' but I don't have the heart to do it."

John tugged her dress. "I thought you said it was cute?"

Jonah picked him up. "You *are* cute. You and Edna both."

John hugged his neck. "Can you take us fishing on the bugs lake sometime? We only went once."

"Buggs Island Lake. I'm going to be busy wiring your house. Don't you want lights in your room?"

John nodded. "I don't like them smelly lamps."

"I don't care for the smell of kerosene myself," Clara said.

Jonah put John down and got a pad and pencil from his truck. "Well, the sooner I make a list of all the supplies we need, the sooner you can stop using those smelly lamps." On the way to the porch, Jonah put the pencil behind his ear. "Some Amish and Mennonites don't allow the members of a community to play musical instruments. I wonder if Samuel would ever let me play the guitar for the Sunday service?"

John scampered ahead and opened the screen door. "What's a guitar, Jonah?"

"It's a—"

Clara shook her head at Jonah, cutting him off. "It's something we have to vote on, Son."

John blinked. "What's that?"

"It's something we do in church."

"Did I ever do it?"

"The adults do it."

"Why can't the boys and girls do it? I might like a guitar if I know what it is."

"I agree," Jonah said, entering the house. Once Clara was inside too, he turned to face her. "I don't like criticizing, but when the Bible says to praise God with musical instruments, I don't understand why it takes a vote to allow it. I've heard of Mennonites playing musical instruments, so what's the problem?"

"The problem is community members wanting to stand out from the rest of us. We're plain people, not fancy folks filled with pride."

Jonah crossed his arms. "I've heard the term 'fancy,' and it's not very nice. In fact, it's judging everyone other than Amish or Mennonite, not a very Christian thing to do." He took the pencil from behind his ear and jabbed it into his shirt pocket. "Maybe I should take my fancy self home and forget wiring your house. I sure don't have to worry about Tess judging me like that."

John pushed Clara's leg. "You're mean, Mama. You made Jonah mad."

"You're too young to understand. It's about

discipline."

"What's that?"

"It's being strong when things tempt us."

"What's 'tempt?'"

"It's like when you want to do something that might hurt you."

"Jonah wouldn't hurt us with a guitar. He loves us."

John's sweet but simple words tore a hole in Clara's heart. This was one of few rare disagreements with Jonah—a disagreement that had bloomed out of something as simple as a guitar. Her eyes filled; tears overflowed and ran down her cheeks. "I'm ... I didn't mean ..." She hurried to the sink and snatched a sheet from a roll of paper towels on the counter. Her shoulder's refused to stop heaving. As much as she loved the Lord and belonging to the Beachy Amish Mennonites, she and the children might be better off leaving them. If they did, she could consider telling Jonah how she felt about him.

"You *should* cry!" John yelled behind her. "You're *mean!*"

"Whoa there," Jonah said. "Don't yell at your mama like that."

"But she was mean to you. Papa said to never be mean to people. He said God loves us all the same."

"Your papa is right, but even adults sometimes get confused about things, okay? Now go apologize to your mama and go to your room so she and I can talk."

"Not till she 'pologizes to you."

"She already has, Son."

At Jonah's "son," a huge sob burst from Clara's throat. For him to be John and Edna's father would be a prayer come true.

"I didn't hear her 'pologize," John said.

"That's true," Jonah said, his voice tender. "But she doesn't have to say it. I know her. She's upset, and people say things they don't mean when they're upset, okay?"

"I guess." John's shoes pattered toward Clara. His hand patted her leg. "I 'pologize, Mama." He paused. "But don't be mean to Jonah no more. Me an' Edna want him to be our papa one day."

His shoes pattered away, fading as they entered the hall. When his bedroom door clicked closed, Jonah's hand fell on Clara's shoulder. Although his touch comforted her, she couldn't stop crying. All she wanted was for him to take her into his arms and confess his love for her.

"Please don't cry," he said. "I'm sorry I got mad, but the last people in the world who should judge others is a group that honors God so much. Doesn't that make sense?"

Although his breath warmed the nape of Clara's neck, it sent a warning chill down her spine. What would he say if she said she loved him, was willing to leave the Beachy Amish Mennonites for him, if she turned and held him even though it was against everything she had been taught? There was only one way to find out. "Jonah," she said, turning to look into his eyes," I lo—"

Gravel crunched in the driveway. Beyond the window over the sink, Noah pulled up in his pickup truck. Clara snatched another paper towel and wiped her eyes. Jonah took the pad from the table and went to a corner to start scribbling on it, sensing, it seemed, the seriousness of Noah thinking the wrong thing. After taking a deep breath, Clara went to the door. "Hello, Noah, I wasn't expecting you." She let him in. "Jonah's taking notes for my electrical work."

Noah's blue eyes darted toward Jonah and back. "I see that." He paused as if he were trying to verify the situation, then leaned close to her ear. "It isn't right for you to be behind closed doors with a man," he hissed.

"John's in his room. He was here a minute ago."

"It still isn't right."

Clara's cheeks burned. "You're here. If Jonah

weren't here, we'd be alone behind closed doors. Besides, Vernon gave him permission to come here after Abram died."

"Well, I suppose that's something." Noah straightened. His eyes narrowed. "Your eyes are red. Have you been crying?"

The last thing Clara wanted was to admit her and Jonah's argument—even if it meant lying to hide it. Otherwise, it might cause another argument, this time between Noah and Jonah. "I was thinking of how Abram dreamed of having the house wired for electricity. Now he isn't here to see it."

Jonah came over from the corner. "Abram knows you, Clara. That means his dreams live on in you and the children. I never got to know him well, but if I were him, I'd feel the same."

"You're English," Noah said, anger in his voice. "How do you know what we feel?"

Jonah slid the pencil behind his ear. "Aren't we all human? Don't we have the same feelings? Don't we have the same hopes?" His kind eyes found Clara. "Don't we all need that one special person in our lives who God sends us?"

Noah snorted derisively. "What do you fancy folks know of God?"

"Please," Clara said, sensing an impending

argument. "You both are my friends." She faced Jonah. "My *dear* friends. It's not right for friends to have hard feelings." She faced Noah. "Jonah's right. Before we became Beachy Amish Mennonites, we were human. That tie should bind us first. Whenever I go for groceries in South Boston at that store that has everything, I see people arguing on the TV display about anything and everything. It's like they can't find the humanity in each other. If anyone should know that's wrong, it's us. We need to set an example and get along with one another regardless of who we are."

"Wise words from a wise woman," Jonah said.

"Well, it took a wise man to help me say them," Clara said, patting his arm. "Go finish your notes." She faced Noah. "What can I do for you?"

Noah waited until Jonah went to another corner and started writing again. "Like I already said, I called home to let my parents know I was coming this week. Papa said your papa hasn't been feeling well. Have you called him lately?"

"I called him and Mama yesterday. They didn't say anything about it."

"It's probably nothing, maybe a spring cold." Noah looked out the window over the sink. "I see you haven't plowed your garden spot yet. Can I do it before I leave?"

The unmistakable sound of John's shoes pattered down the hall and into the kitchen. "Hey, Noah. Can I ride the tractor with you?"

"I don't see why not."

"I see why not," Jonah said, his voice stern. "There's no place for him to sit, so it's not safe."

Noah rolled his eyes. "My papa let me ride with him on our tractor all the time. Why don't you mind your own business and go back to your scribbling?"

Shocked, Clara covered her open mouth with her hand. She had never heard Noah speak to anyone this way.

Jonah came over, his heavy work boots thudding the wooden floor. He stuck the pencil behind his ear again. "Noah, we seem to be like oil and water—we don't mix—but I take people's safety seriously, especially when it comes to Clara, Edna, and John."

Although Noah was tall, he was a bit shorter than Jonah, and he also wasn't as broad shouldered. As Jonah glared down at him, he stepped back. "Look at you, ready to fight like the English do. Unlike you fancy folks, us plain folks believe in solving problems peacefully."

Jonah's nostrils flared. "I believe in whatever it takes to get through to a hard head like yours. You will not jeopardize the safety of Clara or her children. Is that understood?"

John went to Clara and clung to her dress. "Why are they mad, Mama? I just want to ride the tractor."

Jonah knelt beside him. He cupped John's cheek in his palm. "I'm not mad, Son. I just don't want you to get hurt. Tractors are dangerous, okay?"

"Jonah's right," Clara said. "Your papa told you and Edna that very thing once. I guess you don't remember."

"Well," Noah said, "that makes sense." He looked up from John to Clara. "I can still plow your garden if you'd like." He went to the door and opened it. "Let's look at your tractor. I'd like to see the controls."

Since most tractors Clara had seen had similar controls, she guessed Noah wanted to speak to her alone, likely to tell her the real reason he had stopped by, whatever it might be. She followed him outside toward the tractor, but he detoured to the inside of the barn, filled with the aroma of hay for the milk cow and manure that needed to be cleaned from her stall. Over Clara's head, in the rafters, a pigeon fluttered out, startling her, and Noah laughed. "They used to scare me like that when I was a boy."

Glad his temper had faded, Clara's nerves

settled. "I should be used to it by now, as much as it happens."

Noah removed his wide-brimmed straw hat and clutched it to his chest. "I'm sorry about getting angry and saying those things to Jonah. My parents were always strict with their discipline, so it rubbed off on me."

Clara understood discipline. Without it, too many people—Amish and Mennonites included—let emotions rule their lives. Emotions such as love and sympathy were wonderful things, but not when they set discipline aside. She had even heard stories of Amish and Mennonite men mistreating their families with physical violence, which astounded her. If anyone should know better than to harm someone they supposedly loved, an Amish or Mennonite husband and father should know better. She told Noah she understood his concern, but to please allow her to set her own rules concerning her family. "I trust Jonah completely," she added. "I told you how he saved Edna's life when a spider bit her."

"I'm grateful he was here for you." Noah looked away and back. "I just wish …"

In Clara's mind, memories surfaced of their past as teenagers walking home after a Sunday singing. Noah could be passionate one minute and bashful the next, like a moment ago, when he had argued with Jonah and now, as he struggled to say he wished he had been here to save Edna instead of Jonah. Although he had been passionate at the beach, when he tried to convince Clara to court him instead of Vernon, when it finally came down to it, he was also bashful about that. He had been the same as a boy, only holding her hand once as he walked her home. This remembrance set a warm ember of nostalgia in Clara's chest. Yes, that walk had happened about ten years ago, and yes, he could assert himself at times, but now he was just that bashful boy again—that boy whose hand in hers had given her the first glimmer of how it might feel to love someone.

He squeezed the hat's brim. The straw crunched and Clara giggled. "Don't ruin your hat. What's on your mind?"

His cheeks reddened. "I ... well, I don't rightly know. I feel all balled up inside."

For the briefest moment, Clara considered standing on tiptoe to kiss his cheek. The thought shocked her because of her love for Jonah. But what if she only *thought* she loved Jonah? What if she only felt gratitude for all the help he had given her since they had met? No doubt she was attracted to him, but attraction meant very little as the years of a marriage rolled by. Mutual respect and friendship were the building blocks to a blessed marriage, while true attraction meant being drawn to a person's inside rather than his or her outside.

The hat crunched again. Noah's cheeks were now a ruddy red, the color of a sunset just before it sank into the horizon. Clara took his hand in hers, fingers twining. "Do you remember our walk that time, when we held hands?"

"I remember." He smiled, just a hint. "I almost fainted when you let me."

"And you never asked to walk me home again. Why?"

"Well, because—" Noah pulled his hand free and whirled away. "You were my dream, Clara. I told Papa how I felt. He said I should consider other girls because I was too young to set my heart on one. We were only fifteen, so I thought he was right. Then, before I knew it, you had met Abram." He turned to face her. "And now my fears have come back. I saw you kiss Vernon, and it broke my heart all over again, like when you married Abram. I don't begrudge him that because I wanted you to be happy. I just feel like I have a chance at my dream again, but something will ruin it."

As sincere as Noah's confession sounded, Clara understood. Ever since she had begun to believe she was in love with Jonah, even to the point of him being her dream, she had felt like someone would come along to ruin it. At first the rumors said that someone was Lydia, but since he was seeing Tess, the rumors of him and Lydia being engaged couldn't be true. Regardless, her dream was still ruined by Tess's English ways of inviting him to dinner, possible to be alone together. As far as dessert, Clara refused to consider it.

Noah leaned down to look her in the eye. "You sure are thinking hard. I hope my confession didn't make you uncomfortable. I feel better now. I've been holding it in so long, I thought I would pop like a cow about to have twin calves."

Clara sputtered laughter. Then she poked Noah's stomach. "My goodness, that must've been painful."

"Oh, it was," he said, nodding.

A moment passed, then another, then another. Somewhere in the hay loft, a mouse scurried. Outside the open barn doors, a female bluebird swooped down to perch on the fence. She was the first bluebird Clara had seen this spring, but where was her mate?

Noah released his hat with one hand and brought his palm to her cheek. "Do you have any idea how much I care about you? One reason I've been afraid is because you might refuse to court me. Another is how much it upset you to find out about Vernon's past with his wife, so I thought you might not trust another man again. Do you think you can?"

Trust meant the world to Clara. She had trusted Abram enough to love him and have his children. She trusted Noah enough to consider doing the same with him.

But …

The one man she trusted most of all—even more than her own papa—was Jonah. Yes, he was her dream, but now she, as many times as she had told herself the same thing, needed to let that dream go.

Despite the discipline that said to not hold Noah lest it lead to a more intimate embrace, she pressed her cheek to his chest and wrapped her arms around his waist. She thought he might pull away. Instead, he dropped the hat and wrapped his arms around her. His shirt smelled of fresh air. His neck smelled of soap from his morning shave.

Abram! I miss you so much. Is it wrong to think of life with another man? Of children with another man?

No answer. Nothing. Not even the scurrying of a mouse in the hay loft where her beloved husband had fallen to his death.

Did she dare to dream of love again? The answer

terrified her. She might if the man were Jonah.

No ... no.

No! That dream is gone, stolen by Tess. Jonah is now—and never will be—nothing more than my friend.

Daring yet another thing her discipline said was wrong, Clara stood on her tiptoes and kissed Noah's cheek. One day she might be capable of more, but not as long as her dream of Jonah still twined itself around her heart like a vine choking the life out of a tree.

Chapter 3

The next day, done with plowing the garden, Clara parked the tractor. On her way to the house, she waved to John. Sitting on the porch steps, he stood and waved back. "You did a good job, Mama. The dirt smells like fishin' worms."

Clara untied the blue bandana covering her pinned-up hair and wiped sweat from her forehead with it. "Whew, that sun is hot."

Beneath the wide-brimmed straw hat, John's head bobbed up and down. He took a handkerchief from his pants pocket and wiped his forehead too. "I know, Mama. Plowing the garden is hard work."

"Not as hard as planting seeds and bedding plants." Clara folded the bandana and put it in her dress pocket.

John did the same with his handkerchief. "I'm

hungry. Can we have lunch now?"

"Of course we can, growing boy."

In the kitchen, Clara washed her hands at the sink. John pulled a stool over and climbed up to wash his hands too. She then made sandwiches from leftover roast chicken and poured glasses of cold lemonade.

Ever since Noah had told her about Papa not feeling well, she had meant to call home. Unfortunately, between cooking supper last night and bathing the children and herself, then cooking breakfast this morning and taking Edna to school, along with plowing the garden too, time had slipped away.

Done with her sandwich, she refilled John's glass, set a plate of raisin cookies on the table, and went to her bedroom to call home. Several rings later, Mama answered. "Hello, Clara," she said, sounding out of breath. "I was taking your papa his lunch."

The news relieved Clara. If Papa's appetite was normal, he shouldn't be sick. Regardless, a few pointed questions might help her find out more. "How are you and Papa doing? Has he plowed the garden yet?"

"Not yet but soon. You must not remember how Pennsylvania is a little cooler than Virginia this time of year. You could always move back and experience it again."

Clara ignored the reminder of how she should move back home, present at every phone call. At least Mama hadn't mentioned her courting Noah. "Yes, Mama, I know it's cooler there than here this time of year."

"Can I help it if I miss you and the children? Do you think you'll ever come back to stay? I keep hoping Noah will ask us to court you. That would be a start."

"I'm a grown woman with two children. I'll decide who I court."

"Don't take that tone with me," Mama huffed. "I understand you not wanting to leave Abram's grave, but he would want you to be happy instead of living your life alone."

Clara opened the nightstand drawer and took out the quartz stone Jonah had given her at the lake so long ago. "I don't need a man to be happy. I'm perfectly content as I am."

"Blasphemy, Clara, and you know it. The next thing you'll say is you plan to marry that English fellow who drove you and the children here last year. What's his name? I forgot it."

Clara raised the stone toward the window to let the sun shine through it. Light sparkled deep inside its clear surface, illuminating flaws within flaws. People were like that: smooth and perfect on the outside, flawed on the inside. *Thank goodness the Lord helps us recognize our flaws so we can be forgiven, even the flaw of loving someone we shouldn't.*

"Clara, are you there? What's that man's name?"

"Jonah," Clara said, lowering the stone. "His name is Jonah."

"That's a nice Mennonite name. Are you sure he's English? You said his sister's name is Lydia. That's a nice Mennonite name too. Are they Mennonite? Maybe they left their community for some reason." Mama sighed. "I hate to mention it, be we sometimes hear of husbands mistreating their wives and children. Maybe that's why they left."

Clara sighed too. Despite being Beachy Amish Mennonite, Mama tended to the dramatic at times. "No, Mama. If they were Mennonite, Jonah would've told me by now." Time to change the subject. "He's going to finish wiring the house soon. I'm looking forward to not buying wood for the wood stove for heat and just moving a switch to run a heat pump. Air conditioning will be wonderful too."

"What do you think of being alone with him behind closed doors? I don't agree with it at all. You know how English men are, always looking at us because of our red hair. Why, I was getting groceries the other day, and one actually asked me out on a date. The nerve!"

A giggle erupted from Clara. "You poor thing. Did you smile at him before he asked?"

"I asked him to get a bottle off a shelf I couldn't reach. Of course I smiled when I thanked him. It's not my fault he took it the wrong way."

Clara sympathized with her. Men sometimes watched her when she went for groceries too. "Well, I just wanted to see how you and Papa are."

"We're fine. I understand Noah's visiting his parents later this week. Isn't he a nice Mennonite boy, visiting his parents often like nice Mennonite children should when they live far away from home?"

"Yes, that's nice of him." A question bloomed in Clara's mind. "Why were you shopping alone? I thought Papa always took you."

"Oh, he's been feeling tired lately. I told him he was working too hard and not getting enough sleep."

"How do you mean tired?" Clara asked, feeling a hard knot of concern in her chest. "Why isn't he sleeping?"

"I'd rather not say," Mama said, which meant

she was going to say. "Well, since you asked, he's worried about you and the children all alone. Why did you and Abram buy a farm over twenty miles from your community? It doesn't make sense."

Heat from the phone warmed Clara's ear. That's what she got for calling her talkative mama. She moved the phone to her other ear. "We wanted a larger farm than was available near Nathalie. We told you that before we bought it. It was a good price too. Being frugal is important, as you know."

"Being near home and family is more important, as *you* know. Counting you, how many families live there now? Four at the most?"

"Define family."

"A couple, smarty britches."

"There are two couples and three single people—me, Mrs. Yoder, and Noah.

"That's not many. Don't you want any more children? You can't have them if you don't get married."

Despite Mama's repetitious insistence on getting married, Clara *did* want more children. She supposed Noah wanted children of his own, but he had never said. "I better get off this English contraption. I just wanted to see how you and Papa are. Let me know if he doesn't' sleep better. Bye for now."

Clara ended the call and put the phone on the nightstand. What had she done with the quartz stone? She got up to search the bed, then sat as she realized it was in her left hand, clutched to her chest. Its warmth in her palm both comforted and pained her. She was a stone, winter-cold and summer-warm at the same time, all twisted in knots from her feelings for Jonah. Knowing she shouldn't do it, she raised the stone to her lips for a kiss. If Noah returned from Pennsylvania and asked to court her, what would she say? Giving up on her dream of Jonah seemed to be impossible. Then again, nothing was impossible with prayer. She would have to spend extra time on her knees before bed tonight.

After returning the stone to the nightstand drawer, she went to the kitchen to check on John. He touched the plate. "I left you a cookie, Mama."

Sitting across from him, she took the cookie. "I see that, hungry boy. What happened to the rest of them? Those crumbs on your mouth tell me a certain little boy gobbled them all up."

"I had to. The ones I ate first was lonely in my tummy for some more." He touched his empty lemonade glass. "Can I have some milk? I'm still thirsty."

At the refrigerator, Clara couldn't help smiling.

God and her children were her life now. Both gave her joy beyond compare, so would it be so terrible to be a single mother if she couldn't fall in love with another man like she had fallen in love with Abram? *Well,* she thought, filling a glass with milk, *if she couldn't find another Beachy Amish man to fall in love with. Jonah wasn't—and never would be—one.*

She sat across from John as he drank milk. Although Mama's suggestion about Jonah and Lydia being Mennonite was silly, they did have traditional Mennonite names. Clara knew very little about their past. Both were nice, even with Lydia's English ways of going clothes shopping for things she didn't need. Still, her and Alison were great friends, talking on the phone often and going shopping in Clarksville and South Boston. Alison liked Lydia's outspoken manner. Lydia like teasing Alison about men. Samuel once said they used more cell phone minutes than anyone he knew. Once, though, he said their conversations took a somber turn. When Clara asked why, he said he hadn't asked Alison, preferring to not intrude on her and Lydia's privacy.

John took his empty glass and plate to the sink. "All done, Mama. Do you need to buy some seeds for the garden?"

Clara went to a drawer by the sink and opened

it. She *was* getting low in a few items. If they left for the home improvement store in South Boston now, she could buy what she needed and pick Edna up from school at Alison's on the way home.

She wet a paper towel and wiped John's hands and face. "That's a good idea, Son. Let's drive to South Boston and see what we can find."

Thirty minutes later, in the store's parking lot, she was peering into the pickup truck's rear-view mirror to re-pin her hair and secure her kapp. The excitement of planting a garden had thrilled her as a little girl. It still thrilled her now, even to the point of almost forgetting her appearance. Yes, the Beachy Amish Mennonites considered themselves to be plain people, but a person should also be neat and tidy.

Smiling at her from his car seat beside her, John combed his chestnut-brown hair with his fingers. "I'm getting ready too, Mama."

"You sure are," she said, handing him his straw hat. "Now, let's go see if the store has stocked their spring seeds."

As they walked across the parking lot, he took her hand. "What month is it? Papa said to plant in a warm month so the seeds will grow."

"It'll be April next week. It's too early to plant now, but we can get the seeds so we'll be ready. The store doesn't have any plants out yet because it's too early."

Inside the store, Clara pointed out various seed packets and let John put them in the shopping cart. Considering her mental list, she noticed a young couple walking hand in hand toward the patio sets. They took turns sitting in chair after chair, until he pulled her into his lap and they kissed. She wore a diamond engagement ring but no wedding band. No wonder they were so happy: they were looking forward to a life of love together, likely with thoughts of children and holidays and everything that makes a house a home.

John tugged Clara's dress. "What are those people doing, Mama?"

Clara faced him, struggling to think of a way to explain this physical act of affection to him. No doubt the Old Order Amish would say this young couple kissing in public was an example of why the Amish and Mennonites should stay separate from the English. It made sense to a degree, such as how public displays of affection were frowned upon in every Beachy Amish Mennonite community that Clara knew of. At least the couple wasn't groping each other like Clara had seen other couples do. They were simply kissing—now smiling and laughing—and as in love as any Amish or

Mennonite couple ever. Some Old Order Amish might say they were trying to draw attention to themselves, but they couldn't be more wrong. As far as this young couple was concerned, as they gazed into each other's eyes, they were the only two people in the world, exactly how Clara and Abram had felt in the early days of their marriage. Yes, they had attended church at Alison's, had enjoyed the meals afterward, had enjoyed speaking with everyone there, but subtle glances and feather-soft touches of fingertips while passing food made them both feel as if they, like the young couple nearby, were the only two people in the world.

John tugged Clara's dress again. "Well, are you gonna tell me or not?"

Clara pushed the shopping cart out of the aisle and knelt by her son. "They're kissing. It means they love each other very, very much."

John's eyebrows scrunched into a V. "Like you and Papa love each other?"

"Exactly right."

"But I never saw you do that."

"We didn't think it was right to do it in front of you and Edna."

"Why not if it made you laugh and smile like those people? Being happy is a good thing, right?"

Out of the mouths of children, Clara thought. *They*

see things so simply when adults complicate them. "Yes," she said, tapping John's nose. "Being happy is a good thing, but rules are good things too. We're Beachy Amish Mennonite, so we have different rules to live by than other people. I know it sounds complicated, but you'll understand better when you get older." Clara stood. "Let's finish shopping and get Edna. School will let out soon."

During the drive to Alison's house, Clara considered her community's Ordnung. For the most part, they followed the usual Beachy Amish Mennonite Ordnung: Women wore head coverings and plain dresses that didn't emphasize a figure. Married men wore beards, although some trimmed them. English was the regular language unlike the Amish, who, for the most part, spoke Pennsylvania Dutch.

Unlike the Amish practice of having Sunday worship in community homes, the Beachies used churches, but the small community in Nathalie hadn't been able to build a church yet. Clara's community, like other Beachy Amish Mennonite communities, also voted on changes to their Ordnung. Not long after the first families established themselves north of Nathalie, a potential member asked if they would vote to allow him to play a violin during the worship service.

Mrs. Yoder and her husband, the oldest couple at the time, said they would move rather than vote on it. The man had brought his violin and asked if he could play it for the Yoders so they could make an informed decision. When they said no, he promptly packed it back in its case, apologized, and withdrew his request to join the community.

Clara and Abram had smiled at each other at the prospect of hearing the violin. They knew of some Mennonite communities that allowed musical instruments in homes, and had once heard two women singing while one played guitar. The resulting harmony of voice and string had amazed them. Several Bible verses even said to praise God with musical instruments. Vernon had mentioned this to the Yoders, who reminded everyone how their Ordnung said people weren't supposed to draw attention to themselves, as it could be seen as pride. At this, many heads nodded, so Vernon had given up any further discussion.

Mrs. Yoder's husband had died last year, bringing to light their dwindling community, now fewer with Vernon's departure. Other Mennonite and Amish communities were experiencing the same thing, sometimes brought on when young people went on Rumspringa. Clara's former community in Pennsylvania didn't practice

Rumspringa. Regardless, they expected members to join the church through free will as she had. Thank goodness her community didn't practice Rumspringa either. If it did, the children of today might become the English of tomorrow, when the sins of the world possibly appealed to them.

Minutes later, when Clara parked at Alison and Samuel's home, Edna was sitting on the porch, her arms wrapped around herself, likely to ward of the cooling afternoon air. Alison came to meet Clara before she could get to the porch. "John, please go sit with your sister. I need to speak with your mama for a moment." She nodded toward the back of Clara's truck. At the tailgate, she faced Clara. "Has Edna said anything to you about missing Abram?"

Clara thought for a moment. "Well, not in so many words. She and John visit his grave every day. It's natural for them to miss him. I miss him too. Why do you ask?"

"I think she misses him a lot more than you think. If it's warm enough, I let the children eat lunch on the porch. More than once I've seen Edna on the swing Samuel hung from the tree in the yard last week. She's always facing away, and her shoulders are shaking like she's crying. I asked her what was wrong one day. She said she misses having a papa and wants you to marry Jonah."

Alison paused. "I know I've teased you about him, but why would she say that? Is anything going on between you two?"

Clara had to consciously stop her mouth from falling open. "How can you ask me such a thing? He's English and I'm not."

Alison placed a gentle hand upon Clara's shoulder. "That's not an answer. What if you were English or he were Beachy Amish? Would that make a difference?"

"I … you … how can you ask me such a thing?" Clara repeated, too ashamed to say more.

"I can ask you such a thing for three reasons," Alison said, her voice stern. "One is I'm your friend. Another is I'm concerned about your daughter. The third is I want you to find love again one day. I didn't think you and Vernon made a good couple. I doubt you and Noah will make a good one either, but there's something about you and Jonah when I see you together. You have that same look of happiness whenever I saw you and Abram together." Alison shook Clara's shoulder. "It's time to be honest, Clara. Do you have feelings for Jonah or not?"

Clara loved her friend, but her endless questioning had gone too far. Regardless of her feelings for Jonah, she had promised to uphold the rules of her community's Ordnung and to honor God in all things. Yes, she had made mistakes, like going for that ride in Pennsylvania with Jonah, but recognizing those mistakes was the first step toward not repeating them.

Still waiting for an answer, Alison placed her hands on her hips and tilted her head to one side, so Clara would give her one. "I care for Jonah deeply. Wouldn't you if he saved the life of one of your boys? That's what my so-called look is about—admiration for him as a friend."

Alison straightened her head. "Well, I suppose I can see that. Just make sure to talk to Edna. It breaks my heart when she cries."

Clara said she would talk to Edna as well as John, thanked Alison for her concern, and got the children into the pickup. During the drive home, Edna and John said nothing. While sitting on the porch steps, maybe she had told John about Alison catching her crying and added to be quiet about it. Then again, maybe she and John had been secretly talking about having Jonah as a papa all along. He was an important part of their lives, so it might be possible, and John had even said yesterday how he wanted Jonah to be his papa. Alison was right. Clara needed to have a talk with them, and she would do so when they got home.

Chapter 4

Noah climbed into his pickup truck and checked his watch again. Yes indeed, Clara should be on the way to get Edna from school soon, so it would be a good time to have it out with Jonah before leaving for Pennsylvania. Something about the man, other than him being English, was irksome, especially the feeling in the air whenever he and Clara were near each other. Although she was a fine Beachy Amish Mennonite woman, she wouldn't be the first woman of any Amish or Mennonite Ordnung to forsake her vows for a smooth-talking Englisher.

As the miles passed, Noah squeezed the steering wheel and hit the dashboard, then admonished himself for both. His Ordnung called for peaceful solutions to problems. Violence only made things worse, leading to loud words, clenched fists, and no compromises. Still, he didn't trust Jonah. Although Clara said Lydia was his sister, they looked nothing alike. Lydia was slight, with dark, almost black hair. Her eyes were like deep pools of night, the pupils bright stars glittering with malice.

Regret filled Noah. He was being unfair, having hardly spoken to her. What might've happened to her bent arm, and how did she get that scar inside her elbow? After his recent argument with Jonah at Clara's house, he wouldn't be surprised if that fiend of an Englisher had something to do with her injury, as well as how he was fooling Clara into thinking he was so nice. The English did things to get things, and what he might want from Clara infuriated Noah.

At the right turn off the main highway, he took several deep breaths to calm himself. *Forgive me, Lord, for letting my temper get the best of me. I'm doing this for Clara's sake, not my own.*

Minutes later, despite his prayer, when he parked behind Jonah's pickup truck, he was almost shaking with anger. He got out, slamming the door, and Lydia opened the porch door. "Why, hello, Noah, how are you?"

Out of regard to a lady, even her, Noah started to tip his wide-brimmed straw hat but realized he had left it in the truck. He retrieved it, pressed it down on his head, and closed the door again, not slamming it this time.

Lydia giggled. "You Beachy Amish men and your hats. With all that pretty blond hair of yours, why not let the ladies see it?"

Noah tipped the hat. "Beg your pardon, but we dress the same as to not stand out amongst our brothers and sisters."

"Oh, I know all about that, but why do we have flowers if not to admire them? Don't you admire me? I think I'm as sweet as a flower. I bet I could attract even a handsome bee like you." Pursing her lips, Lydia twisted a lock of her thick hair around a finger, and Noah's anger dissipated like fog on a summer morning.

He removed his hat. "Please don't speak to me of such things. It's … it's …"

"Yes?" Lydia asked, looking up into his eyes.

"It's not ladylike." He tore his gaze away from hers to look at the house. "Is Jonah here? I need to speak with him."

"What about?"

Noah refused to say. If Lydia were Amish or Mennonite, he could demand she get Jonah without all the questions. Then she would leave them alone so they could talk. He leaned against the truck.

"Please ask him to come out."

Behind the house, a tractor engine rumbled, getting closer. A huge green tractor, with Jonah driving, rounded the corner, getting closer until it almost touched Noah's bumper. The engine died, and Jonah climbed down. "Something I can help you with?"

Noah didn't like his abrupt tone. He eyed Lydia. "I prefer to talk alone."

"I can take a hint," Lydia said, turning to leave.

When the screen door slammed behind her, Noah faced Jonah. "Before I leave for Pennsylvania, I wanted to suggest you not be alone with Clara at her house. It's not proper."

"Is that right?"

"It is," Noah said, standing straighter to look taller.

"It's a good thing you're suggesting it; that way I can ignore it." Jonah took a step closer. "As far as what's not proper, it's you thinking you can tell me and Clara what to do. Even if you were her husband, I doubt she'd put up with it. She's got more backbone than the average woman, Beachy Amish *or* English." Jonah took another step closer. "As far as what's proper, what matters is trust. It sounds to me like you don't trust Clara."

Noah tried to step back from this huge man, but

his backside hit the truck. "I trust Clara. Who I *don't* trust is you." He waved a hand toward the green tractor. "Look at your fancy tractor. You think that makes you important."

"You just don't get it," Jonah said, derision in his voice. "You're trying to act important by criticizing my choice of tractor. I buy what I need to do my work—nothing more. Furthermore, I trust Clara more than you do. I don't assume she can't handle herself around any man, especially me, her friend and neighbor." Jonah strolled over to his pickup and opened the door. "Now," he said, taking a shotgun from the seat, "do you need something else?"

Noah's knees buckled. From the screen door, Lydia giggled. "Don't worry, Noah. He uses that on crows, not people." She hurried out and took him by the arm, then faced Jonah. "Let me get him in his truck before he faints. I never saw someone's face turn that white that fast."

"That's what he gets for not trusting Clara." Jonah chuckled. "Maybe I should teach her how to shoot. You never know when some idiot might try to tell her who to be friends with."

Lydia turned Noah toward his truck and opened the door for him. "For what it's worth, I admire you for caring about Clara. Still, women like to make their own decisions, and she's no exception." She closed the door and raised on tiptoe to look into the driver's side window. "Have a safe trip to Pennsylvania." She grinned. "I know you want to court Clara, but I wouldn't try it. She needs a man like Abram. I talked to him a few times, and he wouldn't dare pull a stunt like you just did. She would have a fit if she knew you were here speaking for her. No woman likes that at all."

"Well, I care about her and the children. Is that a crime?"

"It is when you think you can speak for her."

"Lydia's exactly right," Jonah said, loading a shell into the shotgun."

Lydia stepped away from the window. "You better get out of here. "You're still pale, but he might take you for a crow anyway."

Noah cranked the truck, backed out of the driveway, and continued to Clara's house to wait.

Since he had moved to Vernon's house, he had been concentrating on her so much that he hadn't thought about making a good impression on the children, which he needed to do if he would be their step-father one day.

Moments later, she and the children arrived and got out of the truck. After pressing his straw hat on his head, he strolled over to Clara and knelt by the children. "Good afternoon … umm." He looked up at Clara. "I feel like an idiot. I forget their names."

"John and Edna." Clara grinned. "John's my son and Edna's my daughter. You know, in case you forgot that too."

Noah offered his hand to John, who eyed it. "What do you want?"

"He wants to shake your hand like grownup men do," Edna said. She grabbed Noah's hand and shook it. "Like that."

John looked up at Clara. "Do I have to? I like Jonah better."

Trying not to frown, Noah stood to face Clara. "I dropped by to tell you goodbye before I left for Pennsylvania."

"What about Jonah?" she asked, more than a hint of curiosity in her voice. "After your argument with him yesterday, I thought you might've come to apologize to him."

"What happened?" Edna asked. "Jonah's our friend."

"It was a misunderstanding," Clara said. "It happens to everybody." She faced Noah. "You really should apologize to Jonah. You are, after all, Beachy Amish Mennonite. You're supposed to know better than to hold grudges." She lightly slapped his arm. "Besides, anyone who expects to be my friend has to be friends with my other friends." She looked down at Edna and John. "You two run inside and have a cookie and some milk while I say goodbye to Noah."

When the screen door slammed behind the children, Noah stepped close to Clara and took her hand. "I hope I mean more to you than a friend."

Clara pulled her hand away. "That depends on what I mean to you. If we were to court and marry, don't think you're getting a woman who'll simply do as a man says. Any man worthy of me will compromise on any issue we have. I also run my own vegetable stand by the mailbox in the summer. People come from all around to buy tomatoes and anything else in season. I make baskets too when I have time. When I can, I go with Alison to sell our items together in Clarksville. If it's on a Saturday, either Jonah or Lydia watch John and Edna for me. They enjoy being there, so don't think I'll let them stay with you if they'd rather stay there."

Noah fought the urge to get in his truck and drive away. Clara was much more independent than when he had known her as a teenager. Regardless, as she looked up at him with her lovely green eyes, he recognized her familiar humor, meaning she might be teasing him, at least to a degree. He took his hat off and clutched it to his chest. "Well, since you like taking charge, ma'am, I was wondering if I could get a goodbye handshake."

Clara looked toward the house, possibly to see if John and Edna were watching. Satisfied it seemed, she stood on tiptoe to kiss Noah's cheek. "Drive safe and make sure to check on Papa. Mama says he's just tired from overwork, but I'd like to make sure." On her heels again, she waved a hand toward the left, where, beyond the cow's pasture, oak and hickory trees grew in abundance, their limbs filling with tiny leaves. "Abram and I have over 100 acres here. Maybe I can talk Mama and Papa into moving here in their old age."

The revelation surprised Noah. Clara's parents had never mentioned moving here. Maybe it was just one of her whims. He opened the truck door. "I better go pack. I'm leaving at first light, and I want to be ready."

Watching him back out of the driveway, Clara waved. What a silly man he was, thinking he could leave with only a handshake instead of a chaste kiss on his cheek. Now the hard part: breaking the news to John and Edna about a possible courtship.

She found them at the kitchen table munching cookies. John drank milk and wiped his mouth on the back of his sleeve. "I don't like that man, Mama.

He didn't even know my name."

"Mine neither," Edna said. "Why was he here?"

"I think I told you already, but you must've forgotten." Clara took a seat across from them. "He was my friend when I was a young girl. He used to walk me home from Sunday singing."

John frowned. "Didn't Papa get mad?"

"I hope you didn't hold his hand," Edna said. "You and Papa said good girls don't hold hands until they get married."

"Do you ever hold Jonah's hand?" John asked. "That would be okay with me. 'Sides, you're a grownup woman now." Another bite of cookie, another swallow of milk. "How old are you, Mama? Are you as old as Mrs. Yoder?"

Edna covered a giggle. "She's not *that* old. Mrs. Yoder's hair is white and she's got wrinkles."

Grinning, Clara shook her head. "I'm sure I'll have white hair and wrinkles in no time with the likes of you two giving me a hard time." She faced Edna. "I knew Noah before I met your papa. I held his hand once."

"Then why didn't you marry him?"

One of Edna's brown curls had come out of her kapp. Clara teased it back inside. "Because I didn't love him."

"He came here yesterday," John said.

Edna crossed her arms. "You didn't tell me that before Mama said so a minute ago. We have to watch out for her. Like I told you, she's got to marry Jonah."

Clara held in a sigh. Talking to these two was like trying to talk a turkey into coming to Thanksgiving dinner. "That makes no sense, Edna. First you say I shouldn't hold a man's hand; then you say I've got to marry Jonah. He's not part of our community, so we can't get married."

"What's 'mmunity?" John asked.

"Our Beachy Amish Mennonite community. When you get older, you'll be baptized into the church. Then you'll be part of our community."

About to drink milk, Edna lowered the glass. "I might not do that. I might love a boy somewhere else and want to marry him. You and Papa always said you love each other. I want to marry a boy because I love him, not because he's baptized."

"I'm not gittin' married," John said. "My wife might not let me go fishin'."

Clara placed her elbows on the table and lowered her head into her hands. What an exasperating pair. What did she expect, trying to explain an adult subject to two children?

"Did we give you a headache?" John asked.

Sputtering laughter, Clara raised her head.

"Almost, but you fixed it by making me laugh."

"It's that Bible verse you taught us," Edna said. "A happy heart is like aspirin."

"Medicine," John corrected. "A happy heart takes medicine." He stuck his tongue out. "I don't like medicine."

Clara laughed again. "Well, both of you are certainly medicine for my happy heart. Now, what if I told you I might court Noah? He cares very much for me, and I'd like to see if we'd make a good match."

Edna took a cookie from the plate. "You said that about Bishop Vernon, and he left."

"We weren't a good match. I want to give Noah a chance. Wouldn't you like someone to give you a chance?"

"Will he take us fishing like Jonah?" John asked.

"I'm sure he would."

Edna washed cookie down with milk. "We don't have to leave Papa and move to where Noah is, do we? You said he lives near Grandma and Grandpa."

"He lives here now. You've seen him at Alison's, at church service."

"Oh."

"Well, we'll just haveta to see how it goes," John said. "That's what Papa used to say."

"He certainly did," Clara said, standing with the empty plate and glasses. On the way to the sink, she felt like she had just answered her baptismal questions all over again. She rinsed the glasses. Or rather, she felt like she had been questioned by the bishop who had asked if she were sure about becoming Beachy Amish Mennonite.

Still, if Noah asked to court her, the children had given their tentative approval. Things were looking up. Now all she needed was for Jonah to finish wiring the house. Then the children could get to know Noah in the glow of electric lights instead of the yellow dimness of kerosene lamps.

As John had just said, *We'll just haveta see how it goes.*

Chapter 5

On the way to the house from gathering eggs, Clara breathed in the brisk morning air. It was a few days after Noah had left, and the last Saturday in March had arrived with a blusterous wind, crisp with a hint of the lingering winter.

To her left, holding a small basket of eggs, Edna hurried along. To her right, John did the same, holding a single egg. "It's too early to get up," he had told Clara when she woke him, to which she replied by telling him how gathering eggs was a daily chore both he and Edna had to learn since they liked eating them so much. Edna said she didn't mind reaching beneath the hen's feathered bottoms, as they warmed her cold hands. John did admit to liking their soft clucks of dissatisfaction at being disturbed, saying they sounded like crickets, and crickets, so Jonah had told him, were good fish bait.

Over the hill beyond the house, Jonah drove his tractor in the pasture. On the front, three metal prongs skewered a large roll of hay as if it were a pork roast. He stopped, lowered the roll and backed away from it. Black angus beef steers lumbered up and started pulling at it, strands of hay hanging from their mouths as they chewed. Jonah waved. Clara and the children waved. He had called Clara last night, saying he would work on wiring the house today since it was Saturday. She almost wished he wouldn't. It was hard enough keeping her feelings for him at bay with him living next door, much less with him in her own home.

The tractor rumbled out of the pasture. Jonah closed and latched the gate and went inside, likely to breakfast.

Clara and the children climbed the porch steps. In the kitchen, she and Edna set their baskets on the counter, and John gave his single egg to Edna. "Cook that for me, woman. I'm the man of this house and you need to do what I say."

Edna took the egg. As she started to crush it on John's head, Clara grabbed her arm. "You will do no such thing, young lady."

"But he's not the man of the house. He's just a silly boy."

Clara set the egg in a basket and knelt before her children. "Son, why do you think women must do what men say?"

"Samuel read it in the Bible. God made women to help men."

"Helping doesn't mean doing everything men say." Clara didn't say the rest: *depending on the man, he might request something very wrong, even in a Beachy Amish community.* She had heard stories of men—even in strict Old Order Amish communities—abusing wives and children. *That is as wrong as wrong gets,* she thought, *especially the way some of those terrible cases were hidden by church elders. If anyone should know better, people who claim to be followers of the Lord should know better.*

"See there," Edna said, poking John's chest, "I don't have to do what you say."

John swatted her hand away. "You will when I'm big."

Clara picked John up and sat him in a chair. She did the same with Edna and sat across from them. It was time to give them a lesson in respect.

Gravel crunched in the driveway, followed by the familiar clatter of Jonah's diesel pickup engine. It ended and the truck door slammed closed. His bootsteps thumped on the porch, and he peeked through the screen door. "Am I in time for breakfast? I see y'all at the table." He entered and came over. "Am I interrupting something?"

"You're a man," John said. "Doesn't Lydia do everything you say?"

Jonah took off his baseball cap and ran his fingers through his brown hair. "Do you see any knots on my head? I'd deserve them if I expected Lydia to do everything I say. We ask each other to do things. If it's reasonable, we do them. That's how people get along, by respecting each other."

"Which is just what I was about to teach them," Clara said.

Jonah sat beside her. "What brought this on?"

Edna picked up an egg. "John said I had to cook him an egg because he's the man of the house and I have to do what he says."

Jonah laughed. "Hmm, not good. What did you do?"

"I was going to give him an egg—on his head."

"I stopped her just in time," Clara said.

Pursing his lips, Jonah faced John. "You love your sister and mama, right?"

"Yeah, but—"

"They love you too. Should we treat people we love like you treated Edna?"

"The Bible says God made women to help men."

"Helping is one thing, Son, demanding is another. The Bible also teaches us to treat people like we want to be treated. Do you want to be treated like you treated Edna?"

"I …" A single tear rolled down John's cheek, leaving a wet trial from his eye to his quivering chin. "I miss Papa."

Jonah leaned near Clara's ear and whispered, "I thought that might be what this is about."

The revelation shocked Clara. She had no idea Abram's absence could cause John to lash out like this.

"I miss him too," Jonah said.

"Did you know him?" Edna asked Jonah, her voice rising with curiosity.

"I sure did. We met before he drove to Pennsylvania one time. He came by the house and asked me to keep an eye on his family while he was gone. Before you know it, he was telling me how God had blessed him with the perfect wife and children. He smiled as big and bright as I had ever seen any man smile. He loved you all very, very much."

John wiped his eyes. "Mama's gonna court Noah. When I think about another papa, I think about you, not him."

Jonah smiled, just a hint, as if he were thinking, *Whenever I think about having children, I think about you and Edna.*

Thank the good Lord he didn't say it, Clara thought. If he had, the children would ask why he couldn't marry her, which would lead to another failed explanation of how Beachy Amish Mennonite's couldn't marry the English.

John got up and came around the table to crawl into Jonah's lap. "Can I pretend you're my papa?" He wrapped his arms around Jonah's neck and snuggled his face into his chest. "Just for a little while?"

Edna hopped from the chair, climbed into Clara's lap, and patted John's back. "I'm sorry I was going to hit you with the egg, okay?"

Not loosening his grip on Jonah's neck, John nodded. "I'm sorry I was mean, Edna. I won't ever be mean again."

Jonah kissed the top of John's head. A silent minute passed. Through the screen door, bluebird song warbled. Jonah leaned toward Clara and rested his head against hers. A tear fell from his cheek, dotting her dress sleeve. One fell from her cheek, leaving a matching circle beside his, dark but filled with joy and sadness at the same time. Yes, she would never marry this wonderful man, but she would never forget this moment for as long as she lived.

More time passed, more tears fell, or were they raindrops of the seasons—or of the years—gone by?

John left Jonah's lap and stood beside him. His tears dried, and he started to grow. Birthdays passed: eight years old, twelve, fifteen. The hint of a moustache darkened his upper lip. He wore ragged blue jeans and a tattered T-shirt. On the inside of his arms, needle marks dotted his skin, evidence of drug use. His skin went ashen. His muscles withered. His ribs protruded from beneath the white cloth like rungs on a ladder. The boyish eyes sank into his skull. Dark-bearded now, he lay in a simple wooden coffin. Beside it, dressed in black, Clara wept.

Edna left her lap and stood beside Clara. Birthdays passed: ten years old, fourteen, sixteen, her body now a woman's body, beneath a fitted skirt and sweater. Lipstick stained her mouth. Earrings glittered on lobes. A snug brassiere pressed her breasts upward, revealing cleavage above the red sweater's low collar. Talking to an English boy on a smart phone, she told him she would sneak out of the house that night. Another boy followed, then another and another. Clara woke to a note that said her daughter was pregnant. She was going to get rid of it and get a job in a city, where the boy was going to take her. Don't call. Don't look for her. Just leave her alone.

Another coffin. More needle marks. So much hope. So much love. So many prayers.

Near the old wood stove, a woman in a plain, blue dress sat in a still rocking chair. She opened the stove's door. No embers glowed. No flames flickered. Wrinkles lined her hand. Blue veins shown beneath parchment-paper skin. Age spots. Arthritis. Swollen knuckles.

A hand reached down through the ceiling—Abram's hand. *It's time to come home, Clara. The children are here and I'm here. We've been waiting for you.*

A hand, red and smoking, reached up through the floor. *She's mine. She failed herself and she failed her children.* The hand grasped Clara's ankle. It burned through skin and flesh until it grasped bone. The smell was nauseating.

Clara stood to reach for Abram's hand, barely brushing his fingertips. His hand pulled away. *He's right, Clara. You failed our children, and you deserve the pits of he—*

Opening her eyes, Clara gasped. "What—?"

"You fell asleep," Jonah whispered. He nodded

toward John and Edna, still snug in their arms. "They did too." His eyes were so blue, like the bluebirds. He smiled. "I've loved you ever since I saw you and these two walking on the road that time. It broke my heart to think of you without a husband, of them without a father. When Abram asked me to keep an eye out for you, I never knew I would fall in love with you. Please marry me, Clara. I'll happily spend the rest of my life showing you how much I love you and John and Edna, and our own children too."

Opening her eyes, Clara gasped. "What—?"

"You fell asleep," Jonah whispered. He nodded toward John and Edna, still snug in their arms. "They did too." His eyes were so blue, like the bluebirds. He smiled. "I better get up and get to work. This house isn't going to wire itself." He kissed John's head. "Time to wake up, Son." He patted Edna's kapp. "You too, sweetheart."

As Edna and John yawned, Jonah and Clara set them on their feet and stood. "I'm hungry," John said, rubbing his eyes. He took an egg from the basket. "Edna, let's make scribbled eggs."

Edna giggled. "It's scrambled, you old sleepyhead."

"How about French toast?" Jonah asked.

"What's that?" John asked.

"It's something I should've made you by now," Clara said, setting a pan on the stove.

On Jonah's belt, his cell phone rang. "It's Lydia," he said, studying the screen. Listening, he stepped away. "Hold on, I'll ask and see." He faced Clara. "Lydia wants to take the children to Clarksville. They're having a nature talk at Occoneechee State Park."

"I suppose," Clara said. "I need to make them breakfast first."

Jonah returned to Lydia. "Have you had breakfast yet? Sure, come on ahead." He ended the call. "She'll get them something at the store on this side of the business bridge. They have breakfast sandwiches."

"A nature talk?" Edna asked, eyebrows rising.

"Is it about fishing?" John asked, eyebrows scrunching.

Laughing, Jonah faced Clara. "I need to take this boy fishing before he grows scales.

Lydia arrived minutes later, said they would have a wonderful time, and for Jonah and Clara to not work too hard on wiring the house. While he gathered tools and wire from his truck, Clara cracked eggs for French toast.

As wonderful as their moment of holding John and Edna had been, her dream of them growing up and dying had been a nightmare. Of course it was a sign from God that they needed a father in their lives, one to help Clara guide them along through life's endless temptations. Time and time again she had heard stories of young people falling into the trap of peer pressure, which could lead to drugs and pregnancy—and too many times, death. It didn't just happen to the English either. Even the Old Order Amish, with their strict rules, sometimes fell prey to the wrong crowd during Rumspringa, and sometimes even before or after Rumspringa. With a good father in the house, the chances of such a thing happening would definitely be lessened.

Jonah made several trips in and out, leaving two rolls of wire, a tool box, and a wide belt with tools hanging from it. He had gone out again a few minutes ago and hadn't returned. Clara placed the last piece of steaming French toast in two plates and went to the door but didn't see him. "Jonah?" she called, raising her voice.

"I'm around here." She rounded the corner of the house. Jonah was standing by Abram's grave, his hand on the wooden cross. Saying nothing, she joined him.

In the barn, the cow mooed, ready to be milked. Over the hill, one of Jonah's bulls bellowed. A cool breeze stirred the oak limbs overhead. Jonah's left hand hung at his side. Clara looked away. If not, the temptation to twine her fingers within his would overcome her. All they could ever be were friends, and it was time to seriously consider Noah as a father for John and Edna. If not, the world and its evils might snatch them away.

Jonah patted the cross. "I can't imagine losing a spouse. How did you deal with—" Smiling, he faced her. "You dealt with it through the power of prayer and through God's peace, right?"

His hand tempted her even more. "Having the children to keep me company helped. Being alone would've been unbearable. I would've asked Mama to come stay with me if that were the case."

Jonah turned all the way around to face her. "I've been enjoying my time with Tess."

"So you say almost every time I see you."

A soft smile answered. "I guess so. She has this way of making me feel comfortable no matter what." A second soft smile. "Like you." The cow mooed again, followed by the bull's bellow. "Lydia's good company, but I'd like kids one day. Tess makes me think about marriage and kids."

"Well, if you think so." Just the thought of Jonah marrying Tess made Clara's legs weak.

"I think so. Maybe one day, though, not soon. Would you wish me well?"

She nodded. "I'd pray for you."

"I pray for you and the children every night. I want the best for you." Jonah chuckled. "And since *I* can't marry you, someone else will have to."

Another breeze blew through the oak branches, this time teasing a strand of Clara's hair from her kapp. She fingered it back into place. "I suppose Noah went home to ask my parents about courting me."

"Do his parents approve?"

"I think so. They were always nice to me."

"Do *you* approve? I remember your doubts about Vernon."

"Because of the drive we took in Pennsylvania that night."

"That's right."

"I think Noah and I will be a better match. We're closer in age, and we've known each other a long time. He wants to get to know John and Edna better too. That means something."

Jonah looked away and back. "I don't care to pry, but we're friends, so I care. Will you marry him if you don't love him like you loved Abram?"

Clara paused, then shrugged. "The Amish and Mennonites value family and community. I might be too old to fall in love like I did when I was eighteen. Maybe love is overrated. It's an emotion, and emotions can get people into trouble. *Like when teenage boys take drugs and teenage girls get pregnant,* Clara didn't say.

"I don't know," Jonah said, breaking a twig from an oak branch. "What you and Abram had wasn't overrated, was it?"

"No, but after a while, life can get in the way." Clara remembered waking to Abram rubbing her back, which led to other things. This happened before the children came along, when the daily chores could be done later. She also remembered washing dishes and his hands slipping around her waist, plus kisses on the nape of her neck. Such times made her feel like a girl without a care in the world. She doubted if she would ever feel like that again. She started to shake her head but managed not to. When she and Jonah were talking and laughing together, she felt as much like a girl without a care in the world as she ever had, and that included when John and Edna were with them. What did that mean?

Jonah tossed the twig away. "Let me get to work. I'd like to finish the wiring in time to get you a heat pump installed before summer. You and the children will love sleeping without sweating."

Clara followed him inside and warmed the French toast. She ate quickly while he dawdled, reading a manual that he said was about new wiring codes in Virginia.

Washing dishes, she thought about Noah. If she could fall in love with him like she had Abram, even to the point of feeling like a girl again, it would be a blessing beyond blessings.

Jonah brought his plate over, thanked her for breakfast, and went to an electrical panel he had installed the last time he was here.

As Clara washed the plate, she considered how Jonah had handled John and Edna's argument about the egg. If Noah could be a father to the children like that, she would be triply blessed. Unfortunately, the only way to find out for sure was if she married him, and she knew that about Jonah now.

Chapter 6

While Jonah continued to work, Clara went to a pile of old chicken manure behind the henhouse. It made the perfect fertilizer for the garden. She filled a wheelbarrow and took it to this end of the garden to spread with a shovel and a rake. When she was done, she would plow it under and make rows with what Abram had called a "three-point-hitch." Thank goodness she had learned to drive the tractor. Not only did she make the garden large enough to feed her and the children and to can plenty of vegetables for the winter, she made it large enough to sell extra vegetables at her roadside stand by the mailbox. Customers came from a ten-mile radius to buy tomatoes, potatoes, and onions. They especially loved her summer squash, green beans, and butterbeans. Many also returned for cantaloupes, saying they were the best they had ever tasted.

After the last load of manure was spread, she paused to survey her work. With the Lord's blessing, her garden would result in a wonderful harvest like it always had, which reminded her of Proverbs 12:1: "He that tilleth his land shall be satisfied with bread: but he that followeth vain persons is void of understanding." Unfortunately, vanity seemed to have taken over the English world. More and more, people needed money and things, like fancy clothes, vehicles, and jewelry, to make them think they were happy. As Clara knew through her Ordnung, true happiness came from gratitude for all of God's many blessings.

Jonah came out for something from his truck and went back inside.

And Clara also knew one of her blessings was his friendship. Yes, as she had told herself time and time again, she needed to start thinking of him as nothing more than a wonderful friend. If not, it wouldn't be fair to Noah when she started courting him.

This revelation surprised her. In the back of her mind, she had never given up hope of being with Jonah, and now it seemed she had. She closed her eyes. *Thank you, Lord, for leading me along the righteous path. It was wrong to think of Jonah as someone I could marry when my Ordnung forbids it. Still, thank you too for his and Lydia's friendship. Despite being English, they have helped me and the children as if they were Amish or Mennonites themselves. Amen.*

The plow was still hitched to the tractor, so Clara turned the manure into the soil. Although she enjoyed its rich, loamy fragrance, an occasional breeze blew diesel exhaust back into her face, making her wrinkle her nose and sneeze. Done with plowing, she used the three-point-hitch to make row after row, each ready for planting when the weather warmed. Now, though, she could plant potatoes, wax beans, carrots, and lettuce. This afternoon would be perfect for it, with John and Edna's help.

As she passed the porch on the way to parking the tractor beneath its shed attached to the barn, Jonah stepped out and walked toward her. He didn't wave to stop her, so she continued on. Beneath the shed, she turned the engine off, relieved at the quiet replacing the tractor's incessant noise. She rose from the metal seat and started to climb down, but her dress hung on the brake pedal and caused her to lose her balance. Headed for a hard fall on the ground, she closed her eyes, expecting a terrible blow to her chest—but it never came. Instead, two arms caught her—Jonah's two arms. Still thinking she might fall, she wrapped her arms around his neck and pressed herself to him. The last thing she needed with all the work around here was to get hurt.

Jonah chuckled. "It seems I'm always around to catch you, Clara. If you stop choking me, I'll put you down."

"I … I'm sorry. I didn't mean to choke you. I thought you might drop me."

"I'd never do that. I told Abram I would watch after you and the children, remember?"

All Clara could do was nod. *Dear God, I don't understand how I can love this wonderful man so much if we can't be together. Please reveal your plan for my life to me soon, whether it be to spend it with Noah or Jonah. If not, I might have a nervous breakdown from all my doubts.*

"Clara," Jonah said softly, smiling the sweetest smile she had ever seen a man smile in her life.

"What?"

He licked his lips. "As much as I like holding you, it's not proper." He leaned over and lowered her to her feet.

A sudden rush of heat warmed her face. "Umm … thank you for catching me." She took hold of his arm and raised on tiptoe. "Consider this from a friend." Her lips brushed his cheek. She quickly dropped to her heels, her hand still on his arm, and looked up into his slightly crinkled eyes. He said nothing and neither did she. As much as she had loved Abram, it seemed she and Jonah were made for each other.

He patted her hand and eased it away from his arm. "I came out to tell you the original wiring for the water pump is the wrong size. To be safe I turned it off. I called the closest home-improvement stores, but they don't have any. The one in South Boston is expecting some tomorrow afternoon. I hope you don't mind doing without running water until then."

The practical news replaced Clara's turmoil concerning her feelings for Jonah. "I suppose I have no choice."

"You're welcome to bathe with me if you'd like."

Clara blinked. "What?"

Jonah raised a hand to cover a smile. "That came out wrong, didn't it?" He lowered his hand. "I meant you and the children can bathe at my house."

"Oh," Clara said, relief flooding her. Just the momentary thought of what Jonah had said had sent heat to her cheeks again. *Dear God, please forgive my wicked thoughts. I have no excuse for them either. I suppose I'm a much weaker woman than I ever realized.*

"Will that be all right?" Jonah asked. "If you'd feel more comfortable bathing at Alison's house, I'm sure she and Samuel won't mind."

Clara recalled when she and the children had stayed with Jonah and Lydia while she was getting over her miscarriage and Edna was getting over her spider bite. At the time, although she had been attracted to him, it hadn't been this strong. It might be a good idea to bathe at Alison's house at that.

She thanked Jonah for understanding, and they walked back toward the house. As they climbed the porch steps, the phone in her dress pocket vibrated against her leg. She told Jonah she had a call, and he continued inside. The screen revealed Noah's number, so she answered. "Hello, Noah. How are your parents?"

"They're well but getting slower as time goes by. As you know, I'm the youngest of my brothers and sisters, so they had me later in life."

"Have you checked on my papa yet?"

"I was about to do that, but … well, my parents would like you to come up here for a talk."

The suggestion puzzled Clara. "That's a long drive for a talk. Can't they use a phone?"

"They don't believe in them except for

emergencies. I've told them over and over how an emergency might be one of them needing medical help, but they won't listen." Noah paused. "They want to talk about us courting."

"I hope they approve," Clara said, somewhat exasperated. "I've known them since we were teenagers."

"They won't say what they want to ask you. It sounds serious. Do you think you can come? Tomorrow would be good."

Clara recalled the terrible traffic around Washington, D. C., when Jonah drove her and the children to Pennsylvania. "I don't care to drive that far. I'd ask Jonah, but he's busy working on the house this week."

Noah blew an impatient breath. "I'd rather he not drive you. Can't you hire someone else?"

"Can't your parents use a phone this time. This is very inconvenient. I'm working on the garden too. I don't have time to go all the way to Pennsylvania for a simple conversation."

Noah blew another breath, this one harder. "A talk about our courtship isn't a simple conversation. You're a good Beachy Amish Mennonite woman, Clara. I want to compromise on this, but there are times when a woman should submit to her husband and do what he says."

Clara glared at the phone. After her and Jonah's talk with the children about treating others with respect, Noah telling her to submit to him was *not* the thing to say. "In case you haven't noticed, Noah, we're not married. And let's get this straight before we start courting, I expect submission to run both ways. Abram and I discussed decisions, and I expect us to discuss them also. If you don't want a marriage like that, tell me now."

Instead of a hard breath, Noah breathed a soft sigh. "You ... well, you're right—*of course* you're right. It's just something about Jonah I don't trust."

"I trust him, that's all you need to know. He's done as much for me as anyone in my community."

"Well, doing for others is a good thing. I won't say anything else about him. Ask him if he can drive you. Oh, you said he's working on your house. Can someone else drive you?"

Behind Clara, the screen door squeaked open. She turned to face Jonah, who pointed at the phone. "I couldn't help hearing. I do need to get your water working tomorrow, but Lydia could drive you. She's going to see her parents in Pennsylvania tomorrow for a few days, and Buck isn't too far out of the way."

Clara told Noah to hold on and palmed the phone. "I thought your parents live in Ohio."

"Um, they moved not long ago. I guess I forgot to tell you."

Clara told Noah the news, adding how she would call him when she knew she would get there, and ended the call.

"Would you like me to keep John and Edna?" Jonah asked.

"I'll ask Alison. That will save you the drive, and you can get my water working quicker."

Jonah went back inside, leaving Clara on the porch, puzzling about whatever Noah's parents wanted to talk about. Unfortunately, it would take a drive to Pennsylvania to find out.

Chapter 7

Clara pointed. "It's the second house on the left. The one with the red barn."

"The barns are always red," Lydia said. "Why not blue or green? Something bright and cheery instead of something that looks like it's on fire?"

"Please don't say that," Clara said, remembering a kitchen fire in her parent's house when she was a child. Thank goodness it was just a grease fire in a pan on the stove, but it still made her run from the house screaming. She didn't like hating anyone or anything, but she hated fires.

Lydia parked behind Noah's pickup truck. "Your Noah sure is a handsome man. If you can't talk his parents into letting you two court, I'll see if I can steal him away from them when we get back home."

When it came to men, like with Alison, Clara was used to Lydia's teasing. She was so different from Jonah, nothing like siblings. Then again, Clara was quite different from her own brother and sister.

Noah's tall figure, blond hair beneath a wide-brimmed straw hat he was putting on, came out on the porch. Wearing dark blue pants, a white shirt and black suspenders, he hurried out to the car as Lydia and Clara got out. "Hello, ladies. I hope the drive wasn't too tiresome." He faced Lydia. "Thank you for driving Clara here. That was very nice of you."

Standing on tip toe, Lydia stretched and groaned. "My shoulders are tight. Do you give good massages? Clara will need those when you get married."

Noah frowned. "What's a massage?"

Lydia turned around. "Put your hands on my shoulders."

"I don't think that's proper."

"Do you want to know what a massage is or not?" Lydia huffed.

Clara covered a grin. "Abram gave them to me all the time. You really should know how."

"Well, since it's for you." Noah placed his hands on Lydia's shoulders. "Now what?"

"You rub and squeeze," Lydia said. "Just be

gentle with those big hands of yours."

Noah did so. "How's that?" he asked. His cheeks turned a glorious shade of red.

Lydia wore her dark hair, which she hadn't cut since last year, in a ponytail. She held it aside and tilted her head. "Do my neck too. I'm all tense from driving."

Noah's mouth opened and closed as if her were a fish out of water. "I uh … I uh …"

Giggling, Lydia turned around. "I do have a nice neck, don't you think? Long and slender and tanned from wearing my ponytail outside?"

Noah let his hands drop to his sides. "Well, I suppose so."

Clara got her suitcase from the back seat. "Thank you for the ride, Lydia."

"No problem. Give me a call when you're ready to go. I'm not on any kind of schedule."

Clara said she would, then waved as Lydia drove away.

"She's kind of …" Noah hesitated. "I can't describe her."

Clara was sure he could describe her neck from the way he was looking at it. She wasn't the least bit jealous of Lydia's flirting with him. Since that was the case, what did it mean?

"Let's get inside." Noah took the suitcase.

"Mama and Papa are waiting."

Although Clara knew Mr. and Mrs. Beiler, she hadn't seen them since before her and Abram's wedding. Like Noah, they hadn't attended the service, which had shocked Clara's family. Honestly, she had been shocked too. It wasn't as if she and Noah had agreed to marry, much less to court, and community families were supposed to join in with the happy occasion.

When Clara followed Noah inside the two-story farmhouse, Mr. and Mrs. Beiler were sitting in two rocking chairs by a fireplace. As still as they were, they resembled stone. Their hair was steel gray. Mrs. Beiler's was covered with a black bonnet instead of a white kapp, yet her hair shown at her temples. A black dress draped her generous body, filled out in old age. On the other hand, Mr. Beiler was thin and wiry, with dark, leathery skin from summers outside working. He wore black pants, a white shirt, and suspenders like Noah.

He led Clara to two more rocking chairs opposite the Beilers. As she sat, she felt like she was about to go on trial for some heinous crime. "Good afternoon, Mr. and Mrs. Beiler. It's nice to see you after so long. I hope you're well."

"We're as well as we've always been," Mrs. Beiler said, her voice as creaky as a rusty door hinge. "At least we were until Noah left us for Virginia."

Mr. Beiler's gray eyes focused on Clara. "We were sorry to hear about Abram. Please accept our condolences."

Although the sentiment pleased Clara, in the months following Abram's passing, she had noted the lack of a sympathy card from the Beilers—*or* Noah. Perhaps she needed to rethink marrying into a family with no more regard for her grief than that. "Thank you," she murmured. "That's very kind."

"We always strive to be kind," Mrs. Beiler said. She took a tea cup from a table at her side and sipped.

Noah's eyes darted at her and back to Clara. "Would you like some tea? I'm sure you're thirsty after that long drive." His voice carried the strain of embarrassment at his parent's lack of cordiality.

She told him no, then faced the Beilers. "You asked me to come here. What can I do for you?"

Mr. Beiler's hand rested on a cane at his side. He pointed it at Clara. "We were hurt when our youngest son moved to Virginia. He lives—lived— closest to us, and we counted on him to help us in our old age. Now you want him to set down roots in Virginia. If you marry him, we need him back here with us. He has a nice house behind your parent's house, just a mile away from here. Before we allow him to court you, you must promise to do as we say."

"Now, Papa," Noah said. "I explained how Clara doesn't want to leave her farm. Abram is buried there. Her community is there."

"And *your* community is here," Mrs. Beiler squeaked. "At least it was until you went chasing after a married woman."

"She is *not* married," Jonah said, his voice stern.

Now we come to it, Clara thought. Not only did Mr. and Mrs. Beiler not care for Noah moving to Virginia, they didn't care for the fact that she had been married before. Perhaps they, through some strict set of rules they had conjured up themselves, thought she was spoiled. Regardless, it was the first time Clara had ever heard of parents rejecting to a son marrying a widow. As far as she was concerned, it needed to be the last.

She stood from the rocking chair. She cared for Noah and believed he could make a good husband and father, or she wouldn't consider courting him. Thank goodness he acted nothing like his parents.

She faced him. "You're a grown man. I understand if you'd rather live near your parents, but you said your brothers and sisters live within a short drive. For myself, I'm a grown woman with my own farm and my own children. No one tells me what to do. I'm as capable of making intelligent decisions as anyone else, is that clear?"

Mrs. Beiler shoved Mr. Beiler's knee. "Make her leave. I've heard enough."

Mr. Beiler's jaw worked back and forth. It seemed his wife was used to telling him what to do, and he didn't like it one bit. Perhaps he admired Clara's spunk, perhaps not, but the truth would come out with his next words.

Settling back into the rocking chair, he fingered the handle of his cane. "I've been married many a year. I never cared for our Ordnung's rule of a wife submitting to a husband." He glared at his wife. "And this is what I get for being entirely too lenient in my own home with her demands."

Jonah's face paled. "Papa, this isn't the time—"

"No, Son, it's *past* time." He faced Clara. "I always admired you, young lady. Jonah told me how you never let him get away with teasing you, but in a good-natured way. I like—well, I used to like teasing my sweetheart too, but I didn't marry her." He faced Mrs. Beiler. "Instead, I married you, you old crone."

Jonah's mouth fell open. "Papa!"

Sensing the worst fight ever in this household, Clara picked up her suitcase. "We'd better go."

Mrs. Beiler was working her puckered lips from side to side. She squinted at Mr. Beiler. "Why, it's been ages since you called me an old crone. If I recall correctly, you called me that right before our goodnight kiss for a few years after we got married."

Mr. Beiler patted her hand. "And it's been ages since we kissed goodnight too. Maybe that's what happened to us. Unlike Noah and Clara, we forgot what it's like to court each other."

Mrs. Beiler worked her way up from the rocking chair. "Let me get us all some tea and some fried apple pies." At the kitchen counter, as she poured tea, her shoulders shook as if she were crying. Clara went to her, and Mrs. Beiler faced her. "Please forgive me, Clara. I *have* become an old crone over the years from bossing my sweetheart. He's a fine man, and I'm ashamed."

Clara patted her shoulder. "Think nothing of it. It's one thing to make a mistake, it's another to realize it and do better. That's what forgiveness is all about."

Mrs. Beiler raised a wrinkled hand and palmed Clara's cheek. "I understand about not wanting to leave Abram." She nodded toward Mr. Beiler. "Alive or dead, if someone tried to make me leave that old coot, I'd be upset too."

After wiping her eyes with a dishtowel and pouring tea and plating the apple pies, she and Clara took everything to the kitchen table, where Noah and Mr. Beiler were waiting. The conversation turned to Clara's farm, the ages of the children, how long she and Noah would court before they married, and how often they could visit. Jonah said if things worked out, they could get married in the fall, as was the tradition amongst most Amish and Mennonites. Clara didn't say, but she felt a bit pressured by such an early date. Years had passed since they were teenagers, so she wanted to get to know him again, but even better than when they were young. She certainly would not marry him until they were best friends. Without friendship, love couldn't flourish, especially not a love like she and Abram had shared. Although she had considered less with Vernon, if there was one thing in life she demanded, it was exactly that.

Done with the tea and delicious apple pie, Clara asked if everyone was finished. Nods followed, so she washed everything, dried and stacked the dishes on the counter, and fetched her suitcase.

Noah kissed his mother's cheek, told his father how happy he was that they had found the love of their youth, and led Clara out to his pickup truck. Inside, instead of buckling his seatbelt, he faced

Clara. "You are a miracle, Clara. I haven't seen them that happy in years."

About to buckle her seatbelt, she stopped. "Colossians 3:14-17. 'And over all these virtues put on love, which binds them all together in perfect unity.' I don't know about you, but I won't live in a household without unity. That means not expecting me to be submissive just because. Does that make sense?"

Noah laughed. "After seeing my papa and mama change so profoundly because of your wisdom, I'll never ask you to submit to me again." He cranked his pickup. "Now let's go tell your parents the news."

Chapter 8

On the way to her parent's house, Clara chewed her lower lip. As amazing as the experience with Noah's parents had been, her parents were another thing altogether.

Noah parked and faced Clara. "That Lydia is something else. I like to tease, but she carries it too far. It was more like flirting."

"You didn't seem to mind." Clara poked him in the ribs. "Did you like rubbing her shoulders? How about her long, slender neck, did you like it when she pulled her ponytail back?"

Noah swatted her hand. "Stop that. It's not proper."

"Listen to you," Clara said, smiling. "You act as if a girl never flirted with you."

"Flirting's one thing, being improper is another.

I expect us to honor our courtship properly."

"And just what do you mean by 'proper,' Mr. Beiler?" She took his hand and laced her fingers into his. "Is this too improper for you?"

"Well, I suppose not." He pulled his hand away. "But it makes me have feelings I shouldn't have until we're married."

Clara unbuckled her seatbelt and turned sideways so she could watch Noah's expression. She had never thought of the question she was going to ask him, but she should have.

His eyebrows raised. "Why are you looking at me like that?"

"I need to ask you something personal, and it might embarrass you."

"I don't know what that might be, unless …" His cheeks flared crimson. "No, Clara. We're not going to talk about that before our wedding night."

Although Clara loved her Ordnung, she didn't care for how couples acted as if some subjects couldn't be discussed, not even among adults. From the stories she'd heard from some of her married friends, their mothers hadn't even prepared them for the marriage bed. Thank goodness her own mother had sat her down and explained the basics. If not, she might've leapt out of the bed and run screaming into the night. Abram said his father had spoken to him about it too, saying to be gentle and loving, and everything would work out. This open attitude from their parents had led to her and Abram growing closer than she had ever thought possible.

Clara patted Noah's hand. "I've been a married woman. Does that bother you?"

"Why should it? You're still the same Clara I've always known."

"What about my having children? I'm a much more experienced woman than you are an experienced man. Has your papa told you about the birds and the bees and what to expect on the wedding night?"

Noah covered his eyes. After a second or two, he opened two fingers enough to peek through. "I've seen farm animals doing that. I suppose the ... uh ... mechanics are the same."

To keep from bursting out in laugher, Clara pressed her lips together. Unfortunately, it wasn't enough, and she sputtered laughter until her sides ached.

Noah crossed his arms. "I don't see what's so funny."

Clara fanned her face. "Mechanics? I'm not a tractor, you silly man."

"I know that."

"I'm not a farm animal either. I expect you to be gentle and loving. Since you haven't been married, you'll have to learn how."

Rolling his eyes, Noah shook his head. "I think I prefer unmarried girls. At least they're shy and quiet. You just blurt out anything and everything."

"I'm a woman, not a girl," Clara said, letting a little anger color her voice. "If you'd rather have some shy girl instead of me, say so now. I expect you to be good papa to John and Edna too. They miss Abram terribly, so you'll need to be patient with them."

The porch door opened. Mama came out and waved. She said something too, but Clara couldn't hear for the closed truck window. "Let's go see what Mama wants."

With Clara's suitcase in hand, Jonah followed her to the porch, where Mama smiled. "I see you've got him trained to carry luggage already. Does he wash windows too? I don't care for washing windows at all. Thank goodness your papa doesn't mind."

Noah looked from her to Clara and back again. "He actually washes windows? That's a woman's work."

"Not in this day and time," Clara said. "Like Mama and Papa, Abram and I shared the work around the house and on the farm. Get inside so I can see Papa."

"Go ahead," Mama told Noah. "I want to speak to Clara first."

Clara didn't like the sound of Mama's voice. She hoped this wasn't about Papa not feeling well.

When Noah went inside, Mama led Clara to the other end of the porch. "Are you sure you want to court Noah? You never explained what happened between you and Vernon."

"I told you enough, Mama. Besides, he was too old for me. I should've realized that to start with."

"Do you think you can love Noah? After all, you married Abram instead of him."

"It's possible, but love takes time. We'll find out when we court." *If only Jonah were a member of my community,* Clara thought, *it would take no time at all to know how I feel about him.*

Mama pressed her hands to Clara's shoulders. "What's that I see in your eyes? I haven't seen that look since you told me you and Abram were getting married. Don't tell me you're in love with Noah already?"

Blinking, Clara stepped back. "How's Papa? Is he feeling better?"

"He's decent," Mama said, taking the bait Clara had given her. "I still think he's working too hard.

With all the plowing and tending to the livestock, he needs to get more rest."

"Get more rest? You both got plenty of sleep when I was here. What's wrong with him exactly?"

"Nothing that spending some time with my grandchildren can't fix," Papa said, coming out onto the porch. "Couldn't you have at least brought John? Edna could've missed a few days of school too." Grimacing, he pressed his hand to his right side. "Oh, that hurts."

"How bad?" Clara asked, studying him. "Do you need a doctor? We can take you."

"It's just gas. Your mama made some fine beans for lunch, and they're kicking in."

"Let's go in," Mama said to Clara. "You didn't come all this way to hear him talk about my beans."

Inside, Clara sat beside Noah, already sitting at the kitchen table. Mama and Papa sat across from them. Papa nodded toward Jonah. "Now then, Mr. Beiler, I understand you want to court my youngest daughter. Is that so?"

"Yes, sir, it certainly is."

"Do you think you can talk her into moving back here to be close to her family?"

"Papa," Clara scolded, "we've been through this already. Virginia is my home now."

"You can't blame me for trying. I understand

about not leaving Abram, but he's passed on and Noah's right here in flesh and bone. You'll have children too, and I'd love to be able to spend time with them before the good Lord calls me home."

Clara was tempted to roll her eyes. Papa certainly knew how to make a person feel guilty, but it wasn't working on her. "We'll visit more often. You and Mama can visit us too."

"A fine idea," Mama said.

"I agree," Noah said to Clara. "With more children, we'll need to add some rooms to the house anyway. We'll add a guest room for our parents at the same time."

Papa snorted laughter. "All four of us can't stay at the same time. That would be a bit crowded."

Without meaning to, Clara twisted her lips to one side, a sign she didn't care for people making her decisions for her. "Look, we're not even courting yet. Let's not talk about more children and adding rooms to my house right now."

"That's true," Mama said. "After all, it's your house to make decisions about."

"Well," Noah said, "it'll be *our* house. You know, technically."

"It's a good thing you don't sound so sure of yourself," Clara said, standing, "or I might call this thing off right now. Mama, it's getting late. What can I help you make for supper?"

Papa pressed his hand to his side and groaned. "No more beans, please."

Mama took Clara to the refrigerator, showed her a chicken casserole, and told her to pop it into the oven, that she had gotten it ready this morning. As Clara did, she couldn't help missing John and Edna. Ever since Abram had passed, they and God had been the center of her world, followed closely by Jonah.

* * *

Supper passed with small talk about the weather and gardening. Papa mentioned buying a new bull to replace his old one. Miraculously, he ate like a proverbial bear, without complaining of the pain in his side again. Noah said he was looking forward to taking John and Edna fishing, that he had found a public use area on the way to Clarksville called Staunton View Park, which overlooks where the Staunton and Dan rivers empty into the lake. He added how it had a picnic area they could use.

His interest in spending time with the children pleased Clara. Time would tell, but he might make a good father and husband after all.

When everyone was done eating, Papa took Noah out to walk the farm. Clara cleared the table and dried dishes while Mama washed. "Noah's a fine young man," Mama said. "Although I respected Vernon as a bishop, I didn't think you two made a good match." Mama gave Clara a dish. "I suppose you noticed how well your papa ate at supper. He *has* been working too hard lately, but I think part of his ailments come from missing you and the children. I'm not trying to make you feel guilty when I say this, but he said it broke his heart when you left for Virginia."

"I'm sorry," Clara said, taking the dish. "I enjoy having my own home and farm. I do quite well selling things from my garden. I have enough room to walk in either pastures or woods. It was mine and Abram's dream to have a place like that."

"Which, along with him being buried there, means you'll never give it up." Mama shared a soft smile. "I understand. I hope you and Noah will be very happy."

In Clara's dress pocket, her phone vibrated against her leg. She stepped away to study the screen and saw Lydia's number. "Hello, Lydia. How's your visit with your parents?"

"Clara. Umm ... something's come up. Would you mind staying the rest of the week? Maybe through the weekend too."

Lydia's hesitation made Clara curious. She usually just said things outright. "Is something wrong?"

"No, it's just … well, it's family stuff."

"I can't ask Alison to keep the children that long. I have gardening to do too."

"I wouldn't ask if it weren't important. I called Alison. She said it's fine."

"You shouldn't have done that," Clara said, trying not to let frustration enter her voice.

"I don't see why not," Lydia said, pressing on. "You know how close Alison and I are. Like I said, I wouldn't ask if it weren't important. Oh, I called Noah too. He said he was going back to Virginia after the weekend, so you'll have to stay anyway. If it'll help, Jonah and I can help with your garden."

Almost like during the grease fire in her parents' house when she was a child, panic gripped Clara. She knew feeling this way was wrong, but she preferred making plans and sticking to them. Still, it was nice of Lydia to offer to help with the garden. If Jonah had time to help too, they could easily get her early crops planted in an afternoon. "Well, it seems I don't have a choice. Just call when you want to leave."

"I will. If things work out, we might leave before the weekend. Thanks for understanding, bye."

Wondering what those "things" were, Clara returned to Mama at the sink and told her of the change in plans. Mama, of course, didn't mind at all, as it would give them time to discuss wedding plans.

Clara took a dish from her. She needed to make courting plans first. That would tell the tale, and if things didn't work out with Noah, she might rather become an old maid than to keep going through all this bother.

Chapter 9

On the way home Sunday, a day earlier than Lydia had originally said, Clara watched the white lines on the highway pass. Unlike their trip to Pennsylvania, Lydia had little to say. Perhaps the reason that had forced her to stay with her parents for longer than she had planned was on her mind.

Clara had enjoyed the time with her own parents, spent visiting neighbors and friends, plus her brother and sister and their families. She also enjoyed supper with Noah and his parents on three evenings. They were much more welcoming and friendly than during their initial meeting, and Clara was glad. The last thing she wanted was in-laws who treated her like an outcast.

On the southern outskirts of Washington, D.C., Lydia's hands, which had been gripping the steering wheel tightly, relaxed. "Thank the good Lord *that's* over. What a nerve-wracking place, even if just driving around it." She glanced at Clara. "I didn't get my license until I was twenty-three, not long after Jonah and I moved to Virginia. I can't imagine you driving through all that traffic. You only drive rural roads from your house to South Boston or Clarksville."

Clara thought it strange that Lydia waited so long to learn to drive. Most English got their license at sixteen. Despite knowing she shouldn't pry, her curiosity got the best of her. "Why did you wait until you were twenty-three to get your license?"

Lydia shrugged. "I was going to learn at eighteen. I was dealing with my arm after that, and it took a while for it to heal after the surgery."

The pink scar on the inside of Lydia's left elbow reminded Clara that she had forgotten if she knew what had happened to it. Regardless, with its uncomfortable angle, she could see how it would stop anyone from learning to drive until it healed, but to wait five years made no sense.

The miles passed. They stopped for a restroom break in Fredericksburg and for lunch on the outskirts of Richmond, eating at a table outside a fast-food place.

Lydia sipped her drink and swallowed. "What

do you think of all the things Jonah does for you? I hope you appreciate them. He's as sweet as he can be, but it would hurt his feelings terribly if you were to turn against him. No matter what, he doesn't deserve that."

About to take a bite of a hamburger, Clara lowered it to the wrapping paper. "Turn against him?' What an odd thing to say. Of course I appreciate him."

"But how much? You may not know it, but he has a tender heart. It wouldn't take much to break it."

"Then shouldn't you be worried about him seeing Tess? If anyone would break his heart, she would."

"And you know that how?" Lydia demanded, accusation in her voice.

"I don't understand her relationship with her-brother-in-law, that's how. It's not proper for them to stay in that cabin in Occoneechee State Park alone."

"Because you think they have a physical relationship even though he's married to Eliza. I bet you'd think that about Jonah and me if we weren't related—how judgmental."

"I didn't say that."

Lydia shook her head. "You Amish and

Mennonites think God only accepts you. I know enough about both to make me sick. Some of the men get away with abusing their wives and children while the bishops and deacons say to just repent and it'll be all right. It's disgusting."

"What's disgusting," Clara said, trying to maintain control, "is a man being the father of two sets of children like Denver is. I wouldn't be surprised if Tess's children are his, and that's why he adopted them."

Snorting with revulsion, Lydia glared at Clara. "You mean like lots of men in the Bible had children from more than one woman? And don't forget about David and Bathsheba. Taking the wife of a loyal soldier and having him killed is one of the most disgusting stories I've ever read. God didn't think much of it either."

"It doesn't make what Denver is doing right."

"What he's doing is being a great dad to all those kids. From what Jonah tells me, he's amazing with them. I could only hope to have a dad like that. Instead, all I get is a—" Lydia looked away and back. "I'm sorry, but I despise hypocrisy. I suppose some Amish and Mennonite men can be forgiven by their wives and children, but I don't see how. To be hurt so terribly by the one person who's supposed to love and protect you makes me want to vomit. In no way is Denver like that, in no way is Jonah like that. They are two of the finest men I have ever known. If he proposes to Tess, she should accept in a heartbeat. I know I would if we weren't related."

Stunned by Lydia's outpouring of sincere feelings, both for Denver and for Jonah, along with her disgust for abuse in some Amish and Mennonite communities, Clara said nothing. Time and time again she had judged Denver and Tess even though God said to let Him judge. Yes, Amish and Mennonite men were capable of some of the worst things imaginable, many times even repeating those things. Although those actions didn't mean all Amish and Mennonite men did them, from the stories Clara had heard, the number was increasing. Something should be done about it, starting with bishops and deacons recognizing the problem. Only then would guilty men consider the consequences of their actions.

She had lowered her head while considering these truths. She raised it to face Lydia, who was wiping tears from her cheeks with a napkin. "Huh," she said, half laughing. "I bet you're wondering where all that came from, especially since I can be such a tease about men." She balled up the napkin and dropped it on the table. "It's like this ... I know the difference between good and bad, and Jonah and Denver are good. Denver, though, is tough. He has to be to deal with having two families. Tess told Jonah how some people have accused Denver of being a terrible person—a pervert to be exact—but they don't know him. He says he doesn't care, that the only thing important to him is all of his loved ones. Anyone who knows him and Eliza and Tess—I mean really knows them—are amazed by the amount of love between them. They're as accepting of anyone as you'll ever meet. That goes for Absalom and Oneita—Tess and Eliza's mom and dad—too. Maybe that's from their Amish background and from their dedication to God. Like the Bible says, treat others like you would have them treat you." With a huge sigh, Lydia stuffed her leftover food into the bag. "I don't know about you, but I'm not hungry anymore." She stood. "Let's go. The sooner I get you home, the better it will be."

In the car again, Clara turned away from Lydia. She had known so little about Jonah's sister, and she now admired her. Not only did she have profound insight into moral dilemmas, she had profound insight into not judging others before knowing them. Then again, like the Bible said, judging was God's job, not mankind's job.

But as the miles rolled by, her words about Jonah seemed like a prophesy of some kind. Clara had no intention of hurting him, especially not to the point of breaking his heart. Except for Papa and Abram, he was the most important man in her life.

Clara closed her eyes.

But what about Noah? Why had his name just slipped her mind as if she had never known him?

Leaning her head against the passenger window, she refused to answer those questions. To do so would betray everything she had ever believed, had ever sworn during her baptismal service to believe, had ever sworn to almighty God to believe.

Tears burned her eyes.

And what does all that mean?

Something terrible is coming. I've known it since Abram's body thudded to the ground beneath the hay loft. Since I saw his neck at the terrible angle that could only mean one thing. Since his wide-open eyes and his last breath wheezing from his lungs told me goodbye. Worse than that, as hard as it is to believe, I've known it since I met Jonah. What is it about him? What is it about Lydia? Just when I think I know them, I realize I don't know them at all.

No, I just broke one of the commandments, I lied about not knowing Jonah. Like Lydia and Tess know, he's one of the finest men they—and I—have ever known. If Tess marries him, they will be as blessed with love as Abram and God blessed me with. Still, it breaks my heart to think of him with another woman. What a fool I am.

Clara fingered tears from her eyes. Her life was about to change drastically, and she had no idea how. She could feel it in her bones, could feel it in her tightening throat, could feel it in the pit of her stomach. Betrayal of the worst kind loomed ahead, yet it hid from her like Abram's coming death had hidden from her.

Dear God, whatever is about to happen, please don't let it be as terrible as losing my kind and gentle Abram. Surround the children and I with your strength and help us through this time. No matter what, I'll never doubt your plans for us again. Amen.

She raised her head from the window and sat back in the seat. Minutes later, she was nodding off. Lydia had insisted they leave early, so Clara hadn't gotten enough sleep.

Sometime later, Lydia woke her. "We just passed the exit to Keysville. We'll be home soon."

Clara almost asked Lydia to drive to Alison's for the children, but it was too much to ask after the long drive from Pennsylvania.

Within twenty minutes, Lydia was parking behind Jonah's pickup truck in Clara's driveway.

Beside it, a huge cardboard box had been cut open and was empty. Carrying a tool box and wearing his toolbelt, Jonah came from the side of the house and opened Lydia's door. "Hello, ladies, you're just in time."

Out of the car, Clara stretched. "Just in time to get over sitting since Richmond."

Lydia closed the car door. "Is everything ready?"

Jonah put the toolbox in the back of the truck. "Pretty much. It was more work than I thought, but we got it done."

"Did you need help?" Clara asked. "You didn't mention that."

Jonah kicked the box. "I needed help to set your new heat pump on a concrete slab yesterday. "I just tried it out and was gathering my tools. Congratulations, your entire house is wired and ready, and you have central heat and air conditioning."

Filled with gratitude, Clara went to him. "I had no idea you were going to do everything. I'm sure it was expensive. Let me know so I can make payments. I can pay more when I start selling vegetables from the garden."

"Oh, we'll work it out. I'm just glad to finish it." As he put the cardboard box in the back of the truck, Lydia took Clara's suitcase to the porch and opened the door. "Well, let's check it out and see what you think."

Clara went in, immediately smelling paint. Jonah came in behind her. "If you smell paint, I removed the sheetrock on the wall where the main panel is to make it easier to run the wiring. I had a contractor replace the sheetrock and paint it." He brushed his fingers along the paint, white and gleaming, below the panel.

Lydia left the suitcase by the kitchen table and returned to flip four switches by the door. Light fixtures on the porch ceiling, the entryway, the kitchen ceiling, and by the hall leading to the bedrooms came on. "How do you like that? No more kerosene lamps."

"I suppose." Clara turned the switches off. "But that means a more expensive electric bill."

Jonah showed her the switches in the all the rooms, plus how to operate the heat pump thermostat. After adjusting it and feeling both hot and cold air come from a floor register a few feet away, Clara sniffed. "Do I smell smoke?" Looking around for the source, she pointed at the ceiling over the main electrical panel, which was constructed of pine boards finished with shellac. "Why is it darker there?"

Jonah closed his eyes and shook his head. "I can't do it, Lydia. It's wrong to lie."

Clara studied the dark streaks on the ceiling. She knelt to touch the hardwood floor and stood. The only reason she would smell smoke, have a stained ceiling, and have a damp floor, was because of a—

Like when she was a child, when the pan of grease caught fire, flames filled her mind. They flowed across the stove and licked the ceiling, and it was all she could do to not run screaming from her home.

Her and Abram's home, the home Jonah had set on fire.

With tears flowing and anger flooding her face in hot waves, she glared into Jonah's eyes. "You set my house on fire?" She faced Lydia. "And you knew about it. That's why you wanted to wait to come back, so he would have time to hide it with paint."

"I told her we shouldn't lie," Jonah said.

"And I told you what Alison told me about that grease fire when Clara was a child," Lydia said. "I knew she would act like this."

Jonah faced Clara. "It's my fault. I replaced the wire I told you about and didn't connect the leads good enough. The fire department got here in just a few minutes and—"

Clara drew back her hand as if to slap him. "The *fire* department?"

"It sounds worse that it was, okay?" Jonah pleaded. "I hired a crew to clean everything and rebuild the wall and paint it. They couldn't quite get the smoke off the ceiling and remove the smell, but it's a lot better than it was. I've been airing the house out since it happened."

Clara couldn't believe this. This was the betrayal she had foreseen. "Exactly how much is this going to cost me?"

"I paid for it myself. My contractor insurance will reimburse me for it."

"Things like this happen," Lydia said. "Be grateful Jonah was here. If not, you might not have a house."

Anger and rage filled Clara. She knew she shouldn't let it, but Jonah had almost burned her and Abram's dream to the ground. If he had, she and the children wouldn't even have a roof over their heads. She stomped to the door and opened it. "You've done enough here. I need you to leave so I can get the children and explain what you've done and how they'll never see you again. Don't ever, no matter what, set foot on my property again."

"That's what I get for trying to make you see how judging people is wrong," Lydia said. "If you keep Jonah from spending time with John and Edna, it'll break his heart. He loves them like they were his own son and daughter. He enjoys seeing them at Alison's on Sundays too."

"You English make me sick," Clara spat. "You go to church a time or two and act like you know God. Along with not coming here, don't attend church at Alison's anymore." She whirled toward Jonah. "If you do, I'll tell them what a hypocrite you are, seeing a woman like Tess."

Lydia took Jonah's hand. "Let's get out of here before I say something I'll regret."

Vehicle doors slammed. Engines cranked. Gravel crunched in the driveway and out to the road. Clara went to the kitchen table and sank into a chair. Everything she and Abram had worked so hard for had almost burned to the ground because of a man she thought she loved. Yes, what a fool she was, and what a fool she had been for trusting him.

She got up and unpacked her suitcase. Should she tell the children what had happened or not? The smoke smell wasn't any worse than with the wood cookstove. They might not notice it, or they might think it was just leftover smell from the cook stove. No, she shouldn't complicate their lives with bad news, and it would be bad enough when they asked why Jonah wasn't visiting anymore or going to church.

Breathing a lung-emptying sigh, she dropped into the chair again. She had actually made things worse with her temper. Jonah wouldn't hurt her or the children on purpose. It was like Lydia had said, one of those things that just happened. Regardless, the situation could be used to explain Jonah's absence. He had finished all his work, so now he had to work for other people. Clara knew how to drive the tractor and tend the farm, so she didn't need him for that either. Yes, it was time to make a clean break from him and to start thinking seriously about Noah. After all, they were now officially courting, so she should act as if nothing bad had happened between her and Jonah and as if something wonderful were happening between her and Noah.

She texted Jonah to say she wouldn't tell anyone what had happened as long as he stayed away from church and from her. His text followed: *Okay, but I wish you'd try to understand.* She texted nothing in return, then left to bring the children home. Maybe their fascination with all the new lights would keep their minds off of Jonah for few days, including spending more time with Noah. With any luck at all, or rather, with God's blessing, they could go on a picnic at Staunton View Park. If they went fishing too, that would even be more fun to take their minds off of Jonah. Who knew when that would happen, though. The garden wouldn't plant itself and was now a week behind. Noah had mentioned planting his tomatoes early, but he needed to plant everything else, so any fun might take a while. Like with the lights, all the work might help keep the children's minds off of Jonah too. Clara certainly hoped so. The last thing she wanted was for them to start asking questions about him., especially questions she didn't care to answer.

Chapter 10

In the garden on a hot Saturday morning in mid-July, Noah filled a basket with tomatoes. He had planted his early, and he planned to surprise Clara and the children with these to slice for hamburgers for their picnic and fishing this afternoon.

He straightened and wiped sweat from his forehead with a handkerchief. It didn't take long for the Virginia heat and humidity to get to a person. If not for Clara, he would rather be in Pennsylvania. When they married, and if he gave her enough time, maybe she would be willing to move back there. Being dedicated to Abram while he was alive was one thing, but being dedicated to him after he was dead and buried was another. First, she shouldn't have had him buried behind the house. It just kept the memories roiling in her mind like water boiling in a pot. Second, she shouldn't be here anyway, not with Jonah living just over the hill.

When Noah and Clara and the children were walking the farm, she always made her way back to Abram's grave. She would touch the cross and whisper a few words. Sometimes she smiled, sometimes she didn't. Then she would look over the hill toward Jonah's house.

For an Englishman, he was decent enough, but what kind of hold did he have on her? It seemed to go beyond the things he had done for her after Abram died. No doubt she was grateful to him for getting Edna to the hospital, but the way she gazed over the hill, like the way she used to gaze at Noah when he was walking her home from a singing, worried him.

In the kitchen, he set the basket on the counter and got his old fishing tackle from a corner of the room. With John and Edna in mind, he had brought the rod and reels and tackle box here on his last trip from home. He hadn't fished in years, doing so as a boy and as a teenager, so the tackle needed sorting and the reels needed oiling. New line from a store in South Boston would keep a fish from breaking it too. The last thing he needed, since he wanted to make a good impression on John and Edna, was for a fish to get away.

Done with those tasks, he washed the smelly oil from his hands. As he dried them, a car drove past the sink over the window and parked beside his truck. To his surprise, Lydia climbed out. Her long, dark hair reflected the sun. Snug blue shorts and a pink T-shirt accented her figure. Noah knew he should turn away but couldn't. Women like her proved how it was best to dress plain. Then again, men shouldn't be lusting after them regardless of what they wore. Trying to ignore the heat in his cheeks from his shame, he went out on the porch as she climbed the steps. "Hello, Lydia. This is a surprise."

"Of course it is," she said, humor in her voice. "I'm sure I'm the last person you expected to come up your driveway."

"Well, I wouldn't say that," Noah said, trying to ignore her tanned legs. "Can I help you with something? I'm getting ready to take Clara and the children on a picnic this afternoon. We'll go fishing too."

"Alison said Clara mentioned it. How's the courting going?"

Noah motioned to one of two rocking chairs on the porch and took one for himself. "It's going well."

Lydia sat also. "Well enough for wedding bells this fall, after the crops are in?"

Noah tilted his head to one side. "How do you know that's when Amish and Mennonites marry, after most of the work is done?"

"Oh, I know a lot about Mennonites. After all, Jonah and I live beside one."

The pink lipstick on her full lips drew Noah's attention. "I didn't know you have a Mennonite neighbor. Is it someone I know?"

Sputtering laughter, Lydia leaned close to tap his arm with her fingertips. "It's Clara. Do you have something else on your mind?" she asked, crossing her legs.

Open-toed sandals revealed pink nail polish. Even her feet were tanned. "You're, uh … your skin is very brown. Do you do a lot of yard work?"

"Garden work too. Like Mennonites, I love the outdoors and gardening, except I don't see how the women wear those long dresses. I'd burn up in the summer in those things. That's why I wear shorts." She recrossed her legs. "I know Mennonite men aren't used to being around women who dress like this. I hope it doesn't bother you." She wet a fingertip and rubbed at a smudge on her knee. "I was kneeling in the garden this morning and missed that spot when I went inside to clean up."

A hard swallow tightened Noah's throat. This woman was a temptress. If she stayed much longer, he'd have to ask her to leave. "Well, to be honest ..."

"Yes?" Lydia asked, recrossing her legs again."

"To be honest, it doesn't bother me."

"Good. It's not a woman's fault when a man can't control himself. Don't you think men should be able to control themselves? They expect women to control themselves around handsome men like you."

Noah swallowed again. No woman had ever told him he was handsome. His mother doted on his blond curls, but that was different. Besides, thinking of himself as handsome was prideful. Lydia was right, though. Both men and women should be able to control themselves. Still, it helped if both dressed plainly. Still too, wearing shorts in summer, at least while working outside, would be much cooler than a long dress and long pants. Some Mennonite communities actually allowed members to wear shorts—even women—as long as they covered the knees and weren't snug. He stood. "I should get ready to see Clara."

Lydia stood too. "I was wondering if you had ever seen a movie."

"Don't you know about the Beachy Amish not

watching TV or listening to the radio?"

"I mean on a computer. Some Amish and Mennonites do use computers and laptops."

"They have movies on computers?"

"You can stream them through the internet or watch them on a DVD. One of my favorites is *The Shunning.* A young woman learns she was given to an Amish couple after birth, and she has to decide what kind of life she wants to live. She was about to marry a bishop too."

Noah frowned. "You mean she wasn't born into the Amish community and no one knew it except the couple who took her?"

"That's right."

"My goodness," Noah said, astonished. "How does it end?"

At the bottom of the steps, Lydia turned. "If you don't think Clara would mind you and I watching it on your porch when you get back from your picnic—you know, so we're not alone in your house to keep things proper—you can find out. What do you think?"

Noah didn't think Clara would mind. After all, she had been around Jonah much more than for just one movie. He told Lydia to come around seven. She drove away, waving through the open car window.

Standing on the porch while returning the wave, Jonah caught sight of his watch and ran inside to change his sweaty clothes before he was late for the picnic.

* * *

At the kitchen counter, Clara sliced the store-bought tomato, which didn't smell anything like a garden tomato. She popped a piece into her mouth. The bland favor didn't compare to a garden tomato either. Although some of hers were turning red, none were ripe, so she had resorted to buying tomatoes for the picnic. Come to think of it, she had to buy the potato chips and lettuce and even the hamburger too, since Noah hadn't mentioned buying anything. Jonah would've insisted on providing everything, like he had when he took her and the children fishing that one time on a pontoon boat he had rented at Occoneechee State Park.

Clara shook her head. She needed to forget Jonah and think about Noah. How many times had she told herself that since he had admitted to setting her entire house on fire?

No, that wasn't fair. Although he had only set one wall on fire, it had *felt* like he had set the entire house on fire. Thank goodness the children hadn't noticed the smoke smell. Thank goodness too for them accepting her excuse for Jonah not visiting, which he was busy with other work. When Clara had told them this, shame from lying had burned her cheeks, and she had prayed to God for forgiveness that night before bed.

Ever since Lydia's accusation about Amish and Mennonites thinking God only accepts them, the words had rung in Clara's mind. Some Amish and Mennonites actually felt this way, which was prideful in itself. Only God knew who He accepted. Anyone who thought differently couldn't be more wrong. All people made mistakes. It was how they repented and overcame them that made a difference to God. Mistakes either made a person stronger or weakened them further. If God dwelt in the heart and soul, they likely would be made stronger. Sometimes, though, like with Clara's dishonesty, she didn't know if she were weaker or stronger. When it came to Jonah, weakness was her main sin.

John came from his room and went to the door, now closed because of the air conditioning, and opened it to peer out the screen door. "Where's Noah, Mama? Isn't today when we go fishing?"

Clara looked at the clock over the stove. "He's a little late. I'm sure he'll be here soon."

Sitting at the kitchen table, Edna slid a container of worms back and forth between her hands. "Why did we have to buy worms? Shouldn't Noah have dug some?"

Clara agreed but didn't say so. "Be thankful the store had them."

John closed the door and joined Edna at the kitchen table. "Why do we have to fish from the bank like Noah said? We could go to the bugs lake park and get a boat like Jonah did."

"It's Occoneechee Park," Edna said. "I bet you can't even say Occoneechee."

"Stop being mean to your brother," Clara said. "That's a hard word."

"A big one too," John said, nodding.

On the kitchen table, Clara's phone rang. She hadn't learned how to use ring tones to identify a caller, so she didn't know who it was. The screen showed Noah's number. "Is something wrong, Noah? You're over thirty minutes late."

"Nothing's wrong. Do you have a cooler? I forgot mine."

"I think Abram has one around here somewhere."

"What about one of those small propane grills? Before I left home, I called Samuel. He said the grills at the park have these big metal grates that rust and use wood or charcoal. I don't want to deal with all that."

"I'm sorry, we don't have a propane grill. We could cover the grate with foil and use wood. I'm used to cooking with wood."

"Well, I don't like to get smoky and dirty. Can you cook the hamburgers before we leave? They won't taste as good, but that's the best we can do. I'll get a grill for next time."

Clara thought her pan-cooked hamburgers were quite tasty, but she did prefer them cooked on a grill. Not only was Noah late, he hadn't offered to buy things and had forgotten things. She held in a sigh. "Maybe we should do this when you're more prepared."

"Me?" Noah asked, defensiveness in his voice.

Trying to avoid a misunderstanding, Clara told him she meant *both* of them should've been more prepared. Then she remembered one of the reasons she chose Abram over Noah: he was always late and was always forgetting things, unlike Abram and—as much as Clara didn't care to admit it—Jonah.

"I'll cook the hamburgers now. I bought fishing worms. I hope you have tackle."

Noah groaned. "I'm not too far from home. I'll go back and get it."

Clara started to tell him again they should go another time, but she didn't want to disappoint

John and Edna. She told Noah they would be waiting and took the hamburger patties from the refrigerator. "Edna, get me a pan."

"Aww, Mama," John whined. "I want mine cooked over a fire like Papa did."

"Me too, Edna said. "They taste better that way."

"I think so too," Clara said, turning a stove eye on. She took the pan from Edna.

When the smell of seared beef wafted about the kitchen, Noah clomped up the porch steps and came in.

"You're late," Edna said.

"*Very* late," John added.

"That's enough," Clara said. "Noah does the best he can." She didn't say the rest: *like he always has done.* "Let's be grateful he's here."

He joined her at the stove. "I'm sorry for only doing 'the best I can.'" He grinned. "Yes, I deserve that. Do you forgive me?"

"I will if you'll get some foil from the drawer by the sink so I can wrap our burgers."

Noah did so. Ten minutes later, everything was loaded in his pickup and they were on the way to the park. After turning onto Highway 15 south, he patted Clara's hand." Did you notice I traded my truck for one with a back seat for John and Edna?"

"Oh, really?" Clara teased. "Will you trade it

back if we don't get married? I might change my mind any minute, you know. I'll put up with a late man, but I draw the line at missing out on grilled hamburgers."

"There's the Clara of our teenage years." Smiling sweetly, Noah glanced her way. "I sure have missed her."

Clara silently agreed, except she missed her happiness from being with Jonah. *Why did I think that? I miss my happiness from being with Abram, not Jonah. He's as far away from me as he can be, regardless of just being over the hill, and all because of my fear of fire. Maybe it's best all that happened. I needed something to get me back to reality. Jonah and I can never be together, so it was best to make a clean break from him and start over with Noah.*

Noah slowed the pickup and turned right. "I wouldn't have noticed this if not for the sign. This park is out in the middle of nowhere."

Several minutes later, after a long drive down a narrow road, they passed a boat ramp, and John asked what it was. "It's where you put a boat in the water," Noah said.

"Why don't you have a boat?" Edna asked.

"Boats are a luxury."

"What's that?"

"It something you want but don't need. We're

Beachy Amish Mennonite. We're frugal."

"What's foogul?" John asked.

As Clara covered a giggle, Noah glanced at her. "This isn't funny, Clara. They need to learn lessons like this."

Clara lowered her hand. "I've taught them about having gratitude for what we need instead of what we want. John, being frugal is not spending your money on things you don't need."

"I don't have any money, Mama. How can I do that?"

"We'll talk about it another time," Clara said as they passed a sign for a picnic area. "We're almost here."

Noah parked near a table with a view of the lake through several trees. Sunlight dappled the water. A soft breeze rustled the leaves shading the area. The children helped carry everything to the table, and Noah and Clara took everything from two bags and the cooler. After Edna said the blessing, making sure to ask God to tell her papa how everyone was all right even though they missed him, Clara put burgers on buns for the children and added mayonnaise, sliced tomatoes, lettuce, and ketchup.

"Where's the onions?" John asked. "Papa liked onions on his hamburger, so I want onions."

"They're too strong for you," Clara said. She added potato chips to his and Edna's plates. "Now enjoy your picnic."

Hamburgers were raised and lowered. Potato chips were crunched. The water through the trees was as beautiful as Clara had ever seen. She had come to love Virginia and wanted to visit the Blue Ridge Mountains eventually.

Noah finished eating quickly and stood. "I'll get the fishing tackle ready while y'all finish. I brought a quilt we can sit on by the water while we fish."

"'Y'all?'" Clara asked. "Are you becoming a southerner?"

He went to the pickup for two rods and reels and a tackle box and returned. "Why not? The quicker I become a southerner, the quicker we can become a southern couple."

Clara cleared the table. Noah gave John and Edna a fishing rod each. Clara got the worms and followed them to the lake, where Noah spread the quilt in the shade of a maple. Using his pocket knife, he cut two limbs in the shape of a V and stuck them into the dirt near the water. Then he baited the hooks with worms, cast them out, and set the rods in the V of the limbs. "There you go," he said to John and Edna. "Keep an eye on the rods. If the tip bounces, you've got a fish." He sat beside Clara on the quilt. A moment later he lay on his side. With his elbow on the quilt, he propped his head in his hand.

Clara did the same thing. What a relaxing day after her turmoil as of late. After she and Abram had been courting a few months, they had talked about people in their pasts. He had considered courting a certain young woman, but before he had hardly thought of it, she started sitting across from someone else after their singings. When Clara told him about Noah, he said he had heard he was a fine fellow, very upstanding. Although he added how he was glad she hadn't chosen him, he said he wouldn't have been a bad choice. His lack of jealousy had won Clara's heart. "God brought us together," he announced. "You can always tell when God brings a couple together by how the look at each other. Their eyes are completely filled with love, and everyone sees it. They are truly blessed."

Yawning, Clara kicked off her tennis shoes and closed her eyes. "I might take a nap. I'm sure someone will yell if a fish bites."

Drowsiness soon took her. Visions of Abram's handsome face passed before her. On the same day they spoke about people in their pasts, they both breached a sad but serious subject. "What would you do without me?" Abram asked. "Do you think it would be easier if we had children?"

Clara knew he meant if he passed away for whatever reason. Just the thought broke her heart, but accidents happened all the time in farming communities. She cupped his cheek with her palm. "If something happens to me, I hope you'll find someone else to love. Life's too short to live alone and in grief. I'll be much happier in Heaven if you promise to do that. Will you?"

He took her hand and kissed its palm. "Will you? I can't imagine resting in peace unless I know you're happy and not grieving over me."

"I doubt I'd ever find someone as perfect for me as you are, Abram. For you, if it makes you feel better, I'll try."

Their shared selflessness had filled her with more happiness than she had ever known. *Thank you, Lord,* she had thought, *for sending me this wonderful man. My cup truly runneth over with love.*

She woke to find Noah smiling at her. "Your babies are napping too."

The late afternoon sunshine had slipped beneath the shade to the foot of the quilt. Lying on their sides facing each other, no doubt warmed like two hound dogs snoozing in the sun, John and Edna were sleeping the sleep of children at peace, secure in the people around them. Clara knew they hadn't caught any fish, or they would've woken her.

"They sure are sweet," Noah said. "He tucked a strand of Clara's hair into her kapp near her ear. "But not as sweet as you."

Like she had done with Abram so many times before, Clara started to pull Noah down for a kiss. *No, it's much too soon for something so intimate. It will have to wait for marriage.*

The thought surprised her. She had expected any thoughts of kissing anyone to be filled with Jonah. Since they hadn't, she might be free of him to move on with her life, even to the point of marrying Noah.

After all, her kind and gentle Abram would approve.

Chapter 11

During his drive home, Noah felt a strange mix of emotions. He had dreamed of being with Clara so long that it seemed the dream had ended now that they were courting. The same thing occurred with the last woman he courted. When she started hinting about marriage, his feelings for her cooled like a thunderstorm cooled a hot summer night. What was love anyway? If it were pure emotion, it could be a problem. The English, who seemed to live on pure emotion all too often, found themselves in all kinds of trouble because of it. Unwed mothers, drug use, and divorce, to name a few, were the results of emotions instead of faith.

Although this was true, his feelings for Clara ran deep because of their shared faith. God would see him through any doubts. If they were meant to be together, it would happen.

Thankful that his house sat far off the road and behind a grove of maples, Noah pulled into the driveway behind Lydia's car. He checked his watch; she was thirty minutes early. As he took the fishing tackle from the rear of the pickup, she took the tackle box. "I don't see any fish."

"We all ended up falling asleep on a quilt."

Lydia grinned mischievously. "It's a good thing John and Edna were there. If not, you might have a scandal on your hands if one of your community members saw you."

Noah took the rods to the porch and leaned them by the door. "Why do you say that?"

Lydia set the tackle box beside the rods. "Because it wouldn't be proper to lie down like that during a Mennonite courtship. Besides, you know how people gossip."

Noah wondered how she knew so much about Mennonites but didn't ask. It was probably because of being friends with Clara and Alison.

Lydia went to her car. She returned with a laptop, a huge bag of popcorn, and a pack of six canned soft drinks. "For our movie." She sat in one of two rocking chairs and pulled the other one close. Noah went inside for glasses and ice for the drinks and sat beside her. She opened the laptop, tapped a few keys, and the movie started.

Despite his interest in an Amish movie, his attention soon went to her long hair, dark like the falling night, flowing across her shoulders. She wore a yellow dress that ended below her knees, plus the same sandals as before. Some kind of sweet perfume on her neck drew him like a bee to a bloom. Clearing his throat, he drew away but still maintained his view of the laptop screen. It was then that he saw a tiny gold cross at her throat, hanging from a chain.

He had never given much thought to English Christians. They had churches of all kinds, but their lifestyles conflicted with the Bible in more ways than he could count. His lips, of their own accord, twitched, signaling how he was trying to solve a problem in his mind. Not all English lived harmful lifestyles. For example, Jonah and Lydia lived on a farm. Although he worked as an electrician, he also raised beef cattle. They sometimes attended church at Alison's, and outside of church, Noah had never heard or seen them do anything unbecoming to Christians. Yes, Lydia liked to tease, but here she was, quiet and calm, enjoying the simple pleasure of sitting on a porch at twilight while learning about the Amish through this movie.

They drank soft drink and munched popcorn in silence. Darkness fell, leaving the soft glow of the laptop screen to illuminate their faces. The movie ended. Noah turned the porch light on, and Lydia closed the laptop. "Did you enjoy it?"

Noah wasn't sure what to think, and his confusion wasn't about the movie. "Why did you want me to watch this movie with you? I don't mean to be rude, but it isn't like we're friends."

Swallowing soft drink, Lydia lowered the glass. "Aren't we friends now?"

"You know what I mean. Why me? Why now?"

"Jonah's off with Tess taking guitar lessons, and I didn't feel like being alone. I thought about asking Alison, but she has her family, so …"

"You don't have many friends?"

"Not really. I'm kind of shy around people I don't know well."

Noah sputtered laughter. "You, shy?"

A moment passed. Lydia rubbed the scar inside her left elbow. "Maybe shy's the wrong word."

Noah had often wondered about the scar and why her elbow was bent at an odd angle. Regardless, her voice, low and somewhat sad, stopped him from asking about it. He really wanted to know more about her, but he didn't care to pry.

She sipped again, then held the glass between

her hands in her lap. Raising her eyes, she softly sighed. "It's a beautiful night. I love listening to the crickets chirp and the breeze rustling the leaves." She faced Noah. "Will you propose to Clara soon?"

Noah didn't hesitate. "I'd like to, but I don't want to rush our courtship. She's been through a lot … you know, with losing Abram. I want her to be sure."

"Because of how Vernon broke their courtship, right?"

"That and I don't want to marry a woman who isn't sure she loves me. It's not fair to her or me, and it's not fair to John and Edna."

Lydia blinked once, twice, and once again. "Why, Noah, I do believe you'd make a wonderful husband. You're caring and kind, and you're very romantic, believing in true love."

Car tires hissed on the road. She waited until the sound faded. "Being Beachy Amish Mennonite, what do they think should be done with Amish and Mennonite men who abuse their family members? I know they're supposed to be forgiven if they repent, but what if they repent and keep doing it? It's bad enough to harm those you love, but I think it's worse to keep doing it when you say you won't."

Looking away, Noah clenched his fists. At home

in Pennsylvania, he had heard of another community where a man abused his wife. They had just gotten married, and he beat her for not keeping the house spotless like his mother kept hers. His wife's mother had died during her birth, so she did the best she could, not having an experienced woman to learn from. Her father loved her dearly. As she was his only child, he wasn't too concerned about the housekeeping. When the young wife told the bishop of the community about the beatings, he told her to do a better job of cleaning the house and had her take lessons from another woman. No matter how well the young woman cleaned or cooked, her husband still beat her. When she told the bishop again, this time with a black eye, he visited the man. The man went into a rage because his wife had reported him and struck the bishop. Then he killed the young women with a butcher knife. The murder had rocked the community. When a new bishop was elected, one who said the wife was at fault, several families joined other communities. After a few months, the rest scattered like dead leaves in a winter wind, leaving the bishop alone without a flock.

Noah didn't think he deserved a flock. For a man—supposedly of God—to blame that suffering young woman for her own death was despicable.

He faced Lydia, who was studying him with narrowed eyes. "Your clenched fists and red face tell me you might have a strong opinion about men who abuse their loved ones."

"I do. No matter who they are—Amish, Mennonite, or English—they belong in jail. Any bishop who can't put himself in the place of the loved ones who are being abused is wrong. If the man truly repents, that's one thing. If his repentance is a lie, that's another." Noah unclenched his fists. "Amish and Mennonites aren't supposed to resort to violence. If my father abused my mother or sisters and wouldn't stop, I might resort to Leviticus, where it says an eye for an eye and a tooth for a tooth. I feel in my heart it's wrong, but it seems violence is the only thing someone like that understands." Noah paused. "Well, I couldn't harm anyone, but I could get my loves ones away from that person. The most important things is to never let it happen again."

Lydia patted his hand. "You're a smart man, Noah, and you have a good heart." She stood with the laptop. "I hope you and Clara will be very happy. Thank you for keeping me company."

As her car passed the maples, the brake lights flashing at the end of the driveway, Noah stood to run his fingers through his hair. In every way imaginable, Lydia had surprised him. Perhaps her teasing was a way to deal with life's burdens or perhaps not, but she was as fine a woman as Clara was.

He put his fishing tackle away, put the leftover popcorn and soft drinks in the kitchen, and got ready for bed. Kneeling beside it in his pajamas, he prayed for many things. Most of all he prayed for God to show him the path to Clara's heart. Without it, he had no idea where his life would lead.

Beneath the cool, air-conditioned covers, he closed his eyes but couldn't sleep. It seemed like a pall of tension hung in the room, like his expectations were about to be shattered into a million pieces. He knew love could do that, like when Clara had married Abram. Still, this was something beyond his past, as if a skeletal claw was reaching from the future to tear his fondest hopes from his heart.

Whatever this fear was clutching at his heart, he hoped he could fight it, hoped he wouldn't surrender. He felt like the happiness of so many people depended on him: his mama, his papa, Clara and the children.

But what about Lydia? Who did she depend on for happiness besides God, evidenced by the gold cross she wore?

Something eerie and strange strained at Noah's senses. He had been here before but didn't understand where *here* was. All he knew was he hoped for happiness for every person important to him: Clara, John and Edna, and Lydia. Even Jonah, as troublesome as he had been by hovering over Clara like a concerned relative, deserved happiness.

Or did he think more of Clara than a relative?

Noah scoffed at the idea. Like Lydia, he was just a kind person with a good heart, even to a fault.

When sleep finally came, visions of Clara's green eyes and red hair and sweet smile filled Noah's dreams. At the moment he knew she loved him, he would drop to his knees and propose.

Chapter 12

Done with Jonah's guitar lesson, Tess offered him a glass of wine for their usual conversation on the dock behind her house, located on the shores of Buggs Island Lake. She enjoyed the hours spent with him, made more productive since Eliza and Denver were willing to keep her kids during the lessons. It also made the time quieter while they sat out on the dock, on a bench she and Denver had built not long after she had moved here.

Jonah declined the wine, so she did too. On the bench, they watched the sun set behind the wooded horizon to the west. As the light transformed a slender strip of low clouds from yellow to orange to scarlet, and finally, to deep violet, the LED fixtures at the edge of the dock came on, illuminating the still water that reflected tiny diamonds of light.

Somewhere in the night, a boat motor whined, its red and green running lights barely visible. In the woods between the edge of the lake and the house, leaves crunched, likely from one of the many white-tailed deer that inhabited the lake subdivision.

Jonah always sat a respectful distance from Tess. He did so now, his left arm resting on the back of the bench between them. Other than her family, he had become important to her. Without a love interest in her life—some cruel people still said that was Denver—she longed for a special man. She didn't think that would be Jonah, but she was willing to try. Along with how much they enjoyed being together, he was great with the kids too. She felt as if a spark burned between them. If she could fan it into flame, who knew where their relationship could lead.

Although all of this drew her to him, he was one of the sweetest men she had never known, no small task considering her relationship with Denver. Jonah possessed a ready smile, a rich singing voice, and a talent for the guitar. His laughter made her laugh, sometimes to tears and an aching stomach. The way he looked at her sometimes created an ache in her chest, as if her heart were melting. She wore her thick, red hair down for him, tucking a few strands behind her ears or pinning it back. The pins usually fell out and the strands usually slipped from her ears. When this happened, he would reach for her temple and stop to silently draw his hand away. More than anything, she wanted him to run his fingers through her hair, to hold her, to kiss her. It had been years since she had felt such an overwhelming desire, but she would draw the line at anything more. She would never make the mistake of letting her emotions carry her to places she shouldn't have gone. Regret concerning her and Denver's past came with many costs. At least it had led to more happiness than she had ever thought possible through a life filled with familial love. As far as Jonah, marriage first, then all the love she and the man of her dreams—if he were him— could handle. First, though, she needed to broach the subject. Unfortunately, she didn't know how to do that. For several weeks now he hadn't been himself: quiet instead of talkative, reserved instead of inquisitive, the ready smile not very ready at all. If Tess didn't know any better, someone had broken his heart. She did know better, because he had never mentioned a love interest. Although he spoke often of Clara and her children, he spoke of Lydia almost as often. When Tess was able to observe him and Lydia together, their affection for each other was obvious, but it seemed more a brotherly and sisterly affection than anything. They never said if they were related, and since they never showed any physical affection, Tess assumed they were siblings. This satisfied her as to Jonah's availability, so there was no time like the present to see if he were interested in a relationship with his guitar teacher.

Another boat motor whined in the night, the red and green lights pinpoints in the distance. Somewhere in the woods, crickets chirped. A warm breeze sprang up, creating tiny waves that lapped against the dock's plastic floats.

Tess loved how her land faced toward the north, up the lake, allowing her a view of both the eastern and western banks and both sunrises and sunsets. Now, as the night grew darker, and no boat motors whined, a hush fell over the lake, followed by a sliver of a fingernail moon rising over the eastern horizon.

Jonah said nothing, though he usually remarked on how pretty the moonrise was here. It's hint of light illuminated his handsome profile, his square jaw, his strong, straight nose. As a teenager, Tess knew she had a devious streak. She wasn't sure why, but she had fought to end it. As if she had wished for it, the warm breeze turned a hint of cold, making her wrap her arms around herself. She faced Jonah. "Whoa, I got cold all of a sudden."

He glanced her way. "The weather on my truck radio said a front is coming in tonight." He pointed at the sky. "I see a few clouds."

Tess scooted close to him. "Do you mind?"

Surprising her, he slipped his arm around her shoulders. "I'm a little cold too." He leaned his head against hers, surprising Tess even more. For a while after she had moved here, whenever Denver walked over to see her, he sometimes held her like this. A few months later, they agreed it wasn't a good idea. Considering their past as lovers, after Eliza had left him, the temptation for more than a simple embrace was too strong.

Tess snuggled into the side of Jonah's broad chest. He carried the aroma or fresh air and the steaks they had grilled for supper. Seconds past. His arm tightened around her. She slipped hers around his waist. Tess felt as if she had died and gone to Heaven. It would take next to nothing to fall in love with this wonderful man, but she didn't want to have her heart broken like when she had given Denver up to Eliza.

"I love your dock," Jonah whispered. "I could get used to this." He paused. "Your kids are great.

I really enjoy being with them."

A thrill ran through Tess. She gave his middle a squeeze. "You are one of the sweetest men I've ever known, Jonah. I really enjoy our time together."

"I do too, Tess, I do too."

Tess's regrets tugged at her heart. She wondered if Jonah had any regrets. One might be that he was almost thirty, and he had never married and had a family. She was twenty-three and longed for what Denver and Eliza had, which was an extremely loving and understanding marriage. Tess herself wasn't sure she would allow her husband to spend so much time with another woman, even to the point of staying overnight in a cabin in Occoneechee State Park. Maybe Eliza allowed it because she knew she could trust her and Denver. After all, Tess had given him up when she likely could have married him. She sighed deeply. That was a past long gone—one never to return. Now she might have a chance at the same love her sister had.

She gave Jonah another hug. "Do you regret not being married? Most people get married earlier than your age. I know you love kids by how you spend time with mine and talk about Clara's."

"Oh, sometimes I wish I had married when I was younger, but I never met anyone that special. Know what I mean?"

Tess knew exactly what he meant. The most special man she knew was Denver. She had dated a few guys, but none came as close to Denver as Jonah did. "I know what you mean. A lot of people get divorced these days too, and I want to be sure of a guy before I marry him."

The breeze grew cooler, and she felt the prickle of goose bumps on her arms. She asked Jonah if he wanted to go inside, but he said he was fine if she was. Sitting here in his arms, she was amazingly fine. "I assume you dated. Do you have any idea why you never met the right woman?"

"You know I'm pretty religious, so that might be it. A few wanted to jump in bed after a few dates. When I said no, they looked at me like I was crazy. Sex has nothing to do with love. Sure, it's part of a great marriage, but marriage doesn't have a chance if the couple isn't best friends first."

Tess snuggled into him again. "I know exactly what you mean."

"Is there a reason you never found the right guy?" Jonah asked. "You told me all about you and Denver and Eliza and how you gave him up, but what about any other guys?"

"The same as you. Too many guys think I'll hop in bed because I'm a single mom. Not only is that disgusting, it's insulting. I've decided to wait until marriage for that. I'm worth it, and any man I marry has to be worthy of me."

Jonah kissed Tess's hair. "I feel the same way, Tess. If I never told you, I think you're amazing."

Tess pulled away and turned sideways on the bench to face him. "As amazing as Clara? You were talking about her and her kids a lot until a few weeks ago. Did something happen?"

"Not really. I told you she's courting Noah, so I've been staying away. I care about her a lot, and she deserves to be happy. If Noah can make her happy, I'm all for it."

Tess looked away and back. "I hope I can find someone to make me happy one day." She raised her hand to Jonah's cheek. "I hope you can find someone to make you happy one day too."

He took her hand from his face. Tess thought he might let go, but he didn't. Instead, he stood and tugged her up with him. "Do you ever feel like you need a hug?"

She nodded. "All the time. When Denver and I were together, I loved his hugs."

"It sounds like you still love him."

"I always will. It's hard to let go, but I think I can if I find the right person." Tess looked up into his eyes. *Please be the right person, Jonah,* she thought.

He opened his arms and pulled her to him. Resting her head on his chest, she wrapped her arms around him and held him as if she were afraid this moment would be their last.

"This is so nice, Tess." He kissed the top of her head. "The last hug I had like this was after Lydia and I moved to my house. She was really grateful for it."

Tess pulled away enough to see his face. "That's because you're such a sweet guy. I'm grateful for you too, or haven't you noticed that?"

He smiled, just a hint in the LED lights, and kissed her forehead. "I've noticed. I hope you know how grateful I am for you."

Tess rested her head on his chest again. "I know, Jonah, I know."

She wasn't sure how long they held each other, but it was long enough for their combined body heat to warm them past comfort. Desire tempted her to kiss him, and not just on his forehead either. *Take it slow,* she thought. *You don't want to mess this up.*

Then, like lightning striking the lake during a summer storm, another thought imploded in her mind.

Like when I gave up Denver to Eliza, I would do anything to make Jonah happy, including giving him up to someone he already loves. But does he love her? With the way he talks about her, he might. If he does, I would step aside without a word because that's how important he is to me.

They continued holding each other, clinging to one another as if they were the two loneliest people in the world.

But if he gives me the slightest hint that he loves me, what a miracle that will be. We'll date until we both say those sweet words, I love you. Then he'll propose and I'll accept. Yes, what an absolute miracle love is, all the sweeter because I learned how to love by loving Denver first.

Chapter 13

At the kitchen sink washing dishes, Clara enjoyed the view through the window. It was the first of October, and the leaves on the maple were tinted scarlet.

Behind her, having finished lunch, Noah, John, and Edna were enjoying slices of apple pie with vanilla ice cream he had brought.

When work around the farm wasn't calling, Saturdays like this had become a routine of sorts. Clara wished Noah had called this time. She had picked the last of her tomatoes this morning to can them this afternoon. Noah said he would help, but she'd rather spend time with him and the children. Not only had she and Noah grown closer since they started courting in the spring, the children were enjoying his company more as well. They still asked about Jonah, but she always said the same thing: "Oh, he's probably busy with his work and those big beef cattle. They eat a lot and need lots of care like you two do." This usually elicited giggles, followed with returning to whatever chore or play they were doing. Still, Clara knew they missed Jonah as much as she did.

Edna brought the three empty plates to wash. She was now seven and in the second grade, getting cuter all the time. "When can I start learning to cook, Mama?"

Pacing her hands on her hips, Clara turned around. "You must be teasing. Every time I ask you to help cook, you turn me down."

"You need to learn," Noah said. "Being a good cook is one of the ways to a man's heart."

"What's another way?" John asked.

Edna giggled. "I think it's kissing, like Mama and Papa used to do."

John frowned. "Yuck. What's fun about mashing your lips together? I do that when I eat. It's not fun, it's just eating."

"Ask the cow," Noah said, winking at Clara. "She mashes her lips together when she chews her cud."

"That's right," Clara said. "She looks like she's wearing green lipstick too." She washed the plates, put them with the others in the strainer to dry, and draped her apron across a chair. "Let's take our walk. It's a beautiful fall day, and the leaves are starting to change colors."

When they all passed the barn, the children, like usual, raced away toward the woods behind the house. Also like usual, Noah slipped his fingers into Clara's fingers. Since the last man to do that was Abram, it made her feel a bit uncomfortable, but she needed to get over it. Noah had hinted about a late fall wedding, and she couldn't disappoint him. The children needed a father too, and it was wrong to not consider them.

At the edge of the woods, John pointed at a fluttering yellow butterfly, and he and Edna ran after it, flapping their arms to mimic the butterfly's flight.

Noah laughed. "I know I'm not old yet, but I wish I had their energy."

Clara said nothing. She felt old and gray, as if she were a widow at the end of her life. She didn't know why she felt this way either. It just seemed to emanate from her in the form of an ache in her heart. It didn't seem to be a physical ailment but a spiritual one. She could work as hard as she always had, but her praying suffered. No matter how hard she tried, a few sentences about her family and the children were all she could manage.

She and Noah had reached the woods. The children were bounding in the tall grass between the woods and the yard. Yes, it was a beautiful fall day, the air crisp, the sun warm, the scent of leaves in the air. Regardless, Clara couldn't enjoy it. She might as well be locked in a glass box for all the good it was doing her.

Noah tugged her to a stop. "Is something wrong? You're quiet like you always are when we take these walks."

He had asked this during their last few walks, and Clara always had the same answer ready. "Oh, I'm just tired from my morning work. You know how it is."

"That's the same thing you said the last four times we walked."

Clara pulled her hand loose from his. "You've never had children. I have to do three times as much work. If it were just me, it would be a lot easier. That's how it is for you."

* * *

Noah's lips twitched. "Oh. I never thought of that." Rubbing his mouth, he studied Clara. When they came back from Pennsylvania, she didn't seem herself. No, it wasn't when they came back; it was the next time he saw her *after* they came back.

Something in her eyes kept them from smiling like they used to, and although a moment of humor might find her, it never lasted long, like in the kitchen when she was teasing Edna about not learning how to cook. She reminded Noah of a strand of barbed wire pulled near its breaking point, and he intended to find out what was wrong, especially before he proposed. He wanted to marry her, but not if their relationship was causing this tension in her. Like he had always thought, he would do anything to make her happy, even if it meant letting her go like he had when she married Abram. In a mix of anger—well, more sadness than anything—he had even considered barging in on their wedding and confessing his love. Fortunately, his morality—as well as his desire for her happiness—had kept him from making a fool of himself.

She continued walking in the tall grass, which swished around her blue dress. At the nape of her neck, beneath the edge of her white kapp, beads of sweat glistened in the sun. Noah trotted to her side but said nothing. The butterfly had escaped the children, and they now ran after a grasshopper that had sprang up from beneath John's feet, whirring and clattering as it tried to escape them.

The scene brought back the memory of Noah

doing the same thing as a young boy. John and Edna simply chased the grasshopper, laughing wildly in their joy. Noah had not laughed when he chased a grasshopper. He thought they were ugly creatures. When he caught them to use as bait for largemouth bass, green liquid oozed from their mandibles, making them appear demonic in his childish mind. This being the case, if he chased a grasshopper for fun and managed to get near it as it sat on a stalk of swaying grass, he would always swat it off and stomp it. He knew this was wrong now, as grasshoppers were one of God's creatures and shouldn't be killed with the same malice he had possessed when he thought about barging in on Clara and Abram's wedding.

From time to time, though, he wondered what would've happened if he had. Then he would scold himself. Clara had been in love with Abram, and no amount of anger would've changed that. Regardless, that anger, like when he had told Lydia how men who abused a wife or child should be punished, sometimes simmered beneath his usual upbeat mood. If Clara were in love with someone else, who knew what might happen. Still, like the proper Beachy Amish Mennonite man, Noah would do the right thing and let Clara go again, but he might have his say to the man who took her.

The grasshopper whirred away, and the children ran to the oak where Abram's wooden cross waited, painted white. Clara joined them, placing a hand on each of their shoulders. She murmured a few words Noah couldn't hear. Then, like she did at the end of all these walks, she faced the hill between her and Jonah's house.

No doubt she was grateful for all the things her neighbor had done for her since Abram died, but her steady gaze seemed to convey something more than mere gratitude: friendship maybe, or admiration. Thankfully, it wasn't love. One of the strictest rules of any Amish or Mennonite community stated that no one may marry outside the church, and that included the Beachy Amish Mennonite church.

Jonah took a step toward her. "Do you think Abram would approve of me?"

Saying nothing, Clara's gaze stayed firmly on Jonah's house.

"Clara, did you hear me?"

John tugged her dress. "Mama, Noah's talking to you."

Clara jumped and whirled. "What? Who's talking to me?"

Noah clenched his teeth. He was tempted to drop to his knees and propose right this minute, but he needed to be sure of Clara, who was again gazing at Jonah's house. To block her view, he moved in front of her. "I'm going home to do a few things. I'll call you later."

"Oh, that's fine. Thank you for coming to lunch."

In his pickup truck, Noah refrained from pressing the accelerator and spinning gravel. Something was going on with Clara, and he intended to get to the bottom of it before this day was over.

On the way home, he alternated between squeezing the steering wheel, clenching his teeth, trying not to speed along Highway 360, and asking God to forgive him for his anger. The Lord's will would be done no matter what, even if it couldn't be seen now.

At home, he dropped into one the rocking chairs on the porch. He could rake the few leaves starting to fall from the oaks lining the driveway if he had a mind to, but he didn't feel like it. Depending on his and Clara's conversation, which he intended to have tonight after the children were asleep, certain decisions—life-changing decisions at that—would have to be made.

As if a ghost had sat in the other rocking chair, it began to rock hesitantly. Then Noah realized a soft breeze had set it in motion. Although Lydia fluttering into his life like a moth around a porchlight on a sultry summer evening had surprised him, their evening spent watching a movie on her laptop had surprised him more. No, it wasn't the movie but their conversation that had surprised him. He chuckled softly. To be honest, and he must be honest, it was the combination of their conversation and her appearance that appealed to him, more-so when she mentioned the problem with Amish and Mennonite men not being punished for abusing their wives and children. Along with her dark beauty, this common thread of justice tugged him toward her like a stitch in one of the quilts his mother often made. Yes, he could forgive someone a terrible wrong, but if the person continued their sin, he or she couldn't be trusted, and trust—as well as faith—was the foundation for a relationship, especially the relationship between a man and a woman when they took the Holy vows of marriage.

Noah removed his wide-brimmed straw hat and ran his fingers through his hair. Vernon had trusted his wife in marriage. Yet, due to no fault of her own, mental illness had ruined their marriage, condemning Vernon to a life without love or family because both Amish and Mennonites offered no reason for divorce. One could understand holding to one's vows, but shouldn't certain circumstances allow it when nothing was gained from forcing a couple to stay married? Certainly they couldn't be positive role models for a Christian home when they were miserable, or, in Vernon's case, it was impossible to be anything but miserable.

Noah blew a frustrated breath. He could ask these questions all day long and nothing would change. They were best left to the bishops and deacons of the church, whose training and dedication to learning the Word of God through the Holy Bible would provide the answers.

He took his phone from his pocket and called Clara to ask if he could come over around nine, when the children were asleep. She meekly replied that he could, likely wondering why, possibly thinking he may propose. No, not at all. Not if his suspicions were true.

Having no appetite, he ignored suppertime when it came, signaled by both his watch and the sun setting to the west. Darkness gathered around him, covering him like a shroud. Now and then a car passed on the road, its tires hissing on asphalt. A cricket at one end of the porch chirped and stopped, chirped and stopped. That once happy sound now aggravated Noah. If he owned a shotgun, he might hunt that cricket as if it were a turkey for Thanksgiving.

At a little after eight, he climbed into his pickup for the drive to Clara's. Twice he had to brake for the glowing eyes of white-tailed deer standing on the shoulder of the highway, watching passing vehicles for an opening in which to dart across without being killed. Depending on how the conversation with Clara went, Noah knew how the deer felt. Their hearts likely pounded in their chests as if death, or freedom from death, were only a few leaps away. Yes, he was bound for a similar destiny, as helpless to control it as when he had found out Clara was marrying Abram.

As he approached Clara's house, he saw Lydia's car and Jonah's pickup at their house. For some unknown reason, he believed Lydia could calm his nerves if he told her all of his fears, all of his dreams, but he didn't dare stop to speak with her.

Mouthing a silent prayer, he parked behind Clara's pickup and knocked on the screen door. Her shadow left the kitchen window. Footsteps padded to the wooden door. She opened both it and the screen door and stood aside so he could come in. He told her he'd rather speak on the porch. She turned the light on and came out. "Hello, Noah." She looked away and back, then went to the end of the porch. Noah had never noticed, but

Jonah's house was visible from there. He joined Clara. On the wooden boards, stained with some kind of preservative, a lighter area beneath her feet evidenced the hours she had been standing here, looking at Jonah's house. Although tears stung Noah's eyes, he had to give her a chance. If not, his regret would join his first regret of not acting before she married Abram, adding the weight of more grief than he could handle to his lonely existence. Yes, God would see him through regardless, maybe even to happiness, but he must make this one last effort.

He sat on the porch steps. Clara came over and joined him. "Did you have something on your mind, Noah? You've never come this late?"

A silent prayer ended the sting of tears in Noah's eyes. Faith would see him through this possible nightmare. He slowly faced Clara. "I've cared about you for so long, I can hardly remember a time when I didn't. When you accepted our courtship, it thrilled my soul, and I thanked God every time I prayed. Now I thank Him for his mercy, because I'll need it if I have to give you up again."

Clara was looking at her hands crossed in her lap. She didn't look at him. "Why … why do you think you'll have to give me up?"

Without warning, a spasm closed Noah's throat.

"Because I don't think you love me."

A single tear slid down Clara's cheek until it stopped at her quivering chin. It hung there, then dropped to her lap. "I'm sorry, Noah, but after Abram, I don't think I'm capable of loving anyone again." A hard swallow tightened the muscles in her throat. She finally faced him. "It was wrong to give you hope. The children and I will be all right. God has gotten us this far, so I know He'll be with us always." She placed a hand on his arm. "I'll always be grateful for how you found out about Vernon. You saved me from marrying a dishonest man."

Unable to take her hypocrisy, Noah stood. "Dishonesty takes all forms, Clara. That poor man just wanted to love and be loved, and he couldn't even have that through no fault of his own. I want love too, but you're lying to yourself about why you can't love me. This has nothing to do with Abram and everything to do with Jonah." To ease his pain, Noah heaved a cleansing breath. "Be honest with me. You owe me that at least."

Another tear quivered on her chin. "I … I don't know what you're talking about."

"It's my most sincere prayer that you don't, that this is a misunderstanding and we still have a chance. To see if any of that's true, I'm going back to Pennsylvania to give you time to think this through. All I've ever wanted is for you to be happy."

"Well, if I pray hard enough, God might help me gain some perspective about Abram and allow me to marry. Isn't that possible?"

"With God," Noah said, not hesitating in the least, "all things are possible." He left the steps for the yard and turned to face her. "I'll leave in a day or two. I won't tell our parents anything about this. If you decide against me, I'll just say it wasn't meant to be."

Clara shook her head once, twice, and once again. More tears joined at her quivering chin and fell to her lap. She raised her red eyes to Noah. "I've never been against you, how can you say that? How can you expect me to forget Abram? Aside from God and the children and my family, he was my life. I can't forget him any more than I can forget how the sun and moon rises and sets, how a summer storm cleanses the air, how—"

"Enough," Noah said, raising his palm toward her to emphasize his interruption. "This isn't about Abram and you know it."

Clara looked down again. "I ... I don't know what you mean."

The temptation to call her a liar trembled on

Noah's lips, but that would be beyond cruel and completely un-Christian. It was clear now: she was so confused with love that even she refused to admit it.

In a sudden burst of realization, more words trembled on his lips. *Are you the liar, Noah? All this time, all these years, have you been in love with Clara, or were you only in love with the idea of loving her, a leftover relic of the time you spent with her as a teenage boy, when emotions and feelings overcome reason, when youth draws a couple together from physical attraction instead of the attraction of the heart?*

He had looked away to ponder those questions. He now faced Clara again—to find her looking at him for the answer to her own question as to what he meant by saying this wasn't about Abram. The sadness in her eyes tore at his heart. The tears overflowing her eyes melted his soul. The realization that he still cared about her enough to marry her crushed his spirit. No, she was beyond him now, but she deserved an answer.

He sat beside her and took her hands into his, both wet from her tears, and gazed into her eyes: brilliant green, begging for understanding.

"Clara, you're capable of more love than I know what to do with, but I know you can't love me. I have no idea what will happen, but like I said a moment ago, with God, all things are possible." He stood at the bottom of the steps and faced her. "I doubt it will happen, but I could be wrong. If you somehow decide you can love me, call me in Pennsylvania, and I'll come back as quick as I can."

Biting his lip to keep from sobbing himself, he drove away into the night. As he passed Jonah's house, he thought he saw Lydia in the window, but since the two-story home was so far away, it might be his imagination. He felt an overwhelming desire to talk with her, or to sit in the shade of a tree by the lake and do nothing but enjoy her company. What that meant, he wasn't sure, but he hoped to discover it eventually, exactly like he hoped Clara would discover the innermost regions of her own heart, regardless of where it led. If what he thought was true, he pitied everyone involved in this nightmare. But like he had said only moments ago, with God, all things were possible.

Chapter 14

Lying in bed the next morning, Clara watched the first hints of sunlight seeping through the window. She had tossed and turned all night, alternating between praying for the strength to be a single mother for the rest of her life and asking God to help her discover if she could truly love Noah. No other option existed—not a single one.

She was past tears, numb with indecision. Thank goodness there was no church at Alison's today. The children could sleep late instead of asking why she looked so exhausted. They would rise soon, though, ready to gather eggs and carry the pail to the cow and sit patiently while Clara showed them how to roll their fingers to get two good streams of milk flowing. With it being October, the milk would steam in the chilly air, matching the twin jets of white bursting from their nostrils as her precious gifts—both from God and Abram—took their turns.

Giving up on sleep, she rose and took her clothes to the dresser mirror. Bloodshot eyes stared back. A pale complexion, more-so than usual, resembled that of a person on their death bed. The luminous cloud of red hair was scattered about her face. Like blood in water, tendrils of it streamed across her shoulders and flowed to her narrow waist. If the white nightgown were black, it would be the perfect shroud.

If not for John and Edna, death might be a welcome thing. Then she and Abram could be together again, and he could comfort her as only he could.

Condemning that thought as nonsense, she brushed and braided her hair, pinned it up at the nape of her neck, and covered it with a blue bandana. A blue dress and white tennis shoes completed her attire. As ready for the day as she could manage, she started to leave her room for the kitchen when her phone vibrated on the nightstand. The sunlight in the window offered enough light to see by, so she left the lamp off as she sat on the bed to study Alison's text: *Call me right away.*

Weary from no sleep, Clara rubbed her eyes as if sand filled them. She loved her best friend, who had also befriended Lydia over the past year, but she could choose the worst times to call. She dialed the number and said good morning without feeling, then waited for Alison to ask why her voice sounded as if it came from the grave.

"I'm sorry to call so early, Clara, but— Well, are you sitting down? I wish I had been sitting down when I heard the news. I almost dropped my phone when Lydia called."

Clara was familiar with her friend's tendency to exaggerate things. "What's going on with Lydia? Did she find another man to gossip about?"

"That's not fair. You don't know her like I do. Well, like I *thought* I knew her. This is something we gossiped about, but we were wrong all the time."

"You gossip, Alison, not me."

"You listen. That's just as bad."

"Fine. What did Lydia do?"

"Are you sitting down? You need to sit down. Please tell me you're sitting down." Clara told her she was sitting on the bed, and Alison thanked God because the news was so shocking. "I don't know how to say this, so I'll just say it. Jonah has proposed to—"

"Of course," Clara said, trying to keep aggravation from her voice. "He's proposed to his precious little Tess. I wondered when it might happen and now it has. I hope they'll be very happy together." Clara didn't say the rest: *They're the perfect couple—he tries to burn people's houses down and she tries to sleep with her brother-in-law.*

Alison blew an aggravated breath. "No, no, that's not it. He proposed to Lydia. They're not brother and sister at all, they're not even related. Like we thought, they've been living in sin all this time right under our noses, even attending church at *my* house. Can you imagine that? Sinning so terribly in my own house? Anyway, she's been telling me things in confidence, but she never told me they weren't related. She and Jonah lived in the same neighborhood in Ohio, except she's Mennonite and he's not. Like I said, she never said they weren't related, she just let me believe it when I mentioned it. Her father beat her and her mother. He even broke Lydia's arm. That's why it's at that angle and she has that scar. Jonah picked her up on the side of the road and took her to the hospital. She's been going back and forth to Ohio, meeting her mother in secret to get her away from her father. Their bishop won't do anything about the beating except to tell him to repent and ask forgiveness. Lydia finally got her mother to move to Harrisburg, Pennsylvania. They haven't officially left the Mennonites, though. Maybe that's why Lydia attended church at my house. Imagine maintaining her faith after everything she and her mother went through, begging for help from their bishop and being ignored. As soon as she got out of the hospital and her doctors released her, she and Jonah moved here to get away from her father. It made Jonah so mad, he said he would like to see how her father felt with a broken arm—or worse. What do you think? I never would've guessed any of that."

Clara hung her head. Jonah and Lydia—she never would've guessed it either. It was just as well. After everything she had gone through, she deserved happiness. If anyone understood that, Clara certainly did. At least he wasn't marrying Tess, the homewrecker. She returned to the phone. "Have they set a date?"

"Not at all," Alison said breathlessly. "She hasn't answered him. She's gone to her mother to see what she says. When she told me all this last night on the phone, she said she never had any serious feelings for him except gratitude for getting her away from her father. She cares for him, but she's afraid what it might do to him if she says no. He's been acting strangely for a while now. It seems as if he's had some bad news, but he won't say what. Has he told you anything?"

Clara said he hadn't, but she was sure the bad news was her telling him to never see her or the children again. All this news, as shocking as it was, was still just as well. She would live life as a single mother, concentrating on God and raising her children in faith, trying to keep them from falling into the trap of the English world with drugs and unwed pregnancies, like in her nightmare.

Saying goodbye, she thanked Alison for calling her, also adding to please keep this news to herself as it wasn't proper to gossip about such serious subjects. Alison agreed, but added how she thought Clara should know.

Done with the call, Clara put the phone on the nightstand. All this time she thought Jonah and Lydia were brother and sister, and they weren't. If not for the leftover numbness from her and Noah's conversation last night, she might've been shocked. All she could do now was to get on with life, which included calling Noah to let him know she couldn't marry him, plus to ask him to keep his word about not telling anyone why.

Still sitting on the side of the bed, Clara blinked over and over again, either trying to rid her eyes of the gritty feeling of no sleep or trying to rid her mind of the one question begging for an answer. Noah seemed to think she loved someone else when she didn't. Why would he think such a thing? The only loves of her life were God, Abram, her children, her family, and her community.

With a huge sigh, resignation filled and emptied her lungs. Time to get on with life—a life without love.

She woke John and Edna. Eggs were gathered, the cow milked. The days passed: canned goods were sold at the roadside stand during the week while the children attended school. When Clara picked them up, Alison refrained from talk of Lydia and Jonah, although she did ask where Noah was. Clara replied that he had gone home to Pennsylvania for the foreseeable future, lying about the reason when Alison asked why: "We decided to end the courtship. We realized we weren't a good fit after all." When she told the same thing to Mama during a phone call, Mama clucked her tongue. "And I was hoping you would marry and move back home. If things keep going like they are, I'll have to gather your brother and sister and all the grandchildren and move there to catch a glimpse of you and John and Edna." She ended the call with, "Come see us when you can, sweetheart. Your papa and I will be praying for you."

The October days slipped by with brilliant autumn leaves covering the ground, both beneath the maple at the front of the house and the oak over Abram's grave in the back. Remarking on the yellows, oranges, and reds, the children raked them into piles, only to jump into them and scatter them and do it all over again. Of course, John was six now and attended school too, coming home to study with Edna until suppertime.

On the first Saturday in November, when frost sparkled in the yard in rainbow hues beneath a glaring sun, Clara came inside with the basket of eggs she had just gathered. Since the children were in school, she let them get an extra hour of sleep on Saturday. When she told them about ending the courtship with Noah, they simply looked at each other as if they shared a secret and went back to their homework. Clara wasn't surprised. Although Noah was a fine man and fine person, he never lived up to the children's standards when it came to Abram.

As far as Jonah and Lydia's engagement, Clara didn't ask Alison about it, and Alison didn't mention it, which was fine with Clara. She even refused to look toward his house or driveway when she was in the yard or driving by. *Let old dreams turned nightmares fade into the past where they belong,* she often chided herself. *I'm satisfied with my lot in life. God has given me everything I need.*

But there were times at night, mostly toward dawn, when she would slide her hand to the other side of the bed, where nothing but cold sheets met her warm hand. Soft weeping transformed into hiccupping sobs, forcing her to press her face into her pillow to keep the children from running in and asking what was wrong.

These were the times when she questioned what love was, what rules were, what morals bound her to Beachy Amish Mennonite customs. Before an answer would form on her lips, she would wipe her face, dry her eyes, and tell herself to stop being a silly school girl and get on with the business of being an adult.

As she was about to break several fresh eggs to scramble, the sound of a vehicle engine came down the driveway and stopped beside the house. She looked out the window over the sink. In a blue dress and black coat, adjusting her white kapp, her breath pluming before her face, Alison strode toward the door, knocked and entered. "I had to come tell you this. You wouldn't believe me over the phone."

Clara started to ask what the difference was

between this news and the news of Jonah proposing to Lydia but didn't. It would only prolong the conversation. "It's nice to see you too, Alison," she said, trying and failing to keep sarcasm from her voice. Regretting it, she offered scrambled eggs, as she was about to cook some.

"Ugh, you'd criticize me at your own funeral. Noah and Lydia are courting."

Clara's mouth fell open. "What about Jonah proposing to her?"

"I just got off the phone with her—she turned him down two weeks ago, after she and Noah started courting. She said they're keeping it to themselves for now, but I thought you should know. I also thought you should know this—she said she hasn't heard from Jonah since then, and he hasn't returned her calls. I stopped by on the way here. He won't come to the door even though his truck is there. Samuel said he hasn't seen him around town, and he's worried about him."

Dropping into a chair at the table, Clara said nothing. *Noah and Lydia? I never would've guessed it. Poor Jonah, now he knows how it feels to be alone and without love like I do.*

Alison sat across from her. "You need to check on Jonah. He might answer the door for you."

"Why should I do that? He's an adult. He should

be able to handle losing Lydia like—"

"Like you handled losing Abram?" Alison interrupted. "As I recall, the only reason you handled it as well as you did is because of Jonah. Look at everything he did for you. He plowed your garden. He saved Edna's life when that spider bit her. He let you stay with him and Lydia while you got over your miscarriage. He paid your hospital bills. He gave you his old refrigerator. He wired your house." Pausing, Alison snapped her fingers. "He even gave you Lydia's old phone and bought you that propane stove and installed it. What's wrong with you, Clara? He's helped you more than anyone in our community has, and you won't even go check on him?"

"He didn't give me the phone, Lydia did."

"He suggested it to Lydia. She told me about the propane stove. She saw the receipt on his desk. She also saw him writing checks to the hospital. When she asked him about both, he said he was only doing what Abram asked him to do, to watch out for you and the children if something happened to him. I think it's more than that, although I don't know what. He never had any siblings, so maybe you feel like a sister to him." In a flurry of blue dress and black coat, Alison stood. "Are you going to check on him, or do I have to drag you there myself? Samuel's fixing the boy's breakfasts, so I'll scramble eggs for John and Edna while you're gone and tell them what you're doing. Take all the time you need, but call if it takes more than an hour. If you want me to, I'll take John and Edna home with me. Jonah might need serious help, and you're just the one to give it to him. If nothing else, after everything he's done for you, you owe it him. If that's not enough of a reason, consider it the Christian thing to do." Alison got up and hung her coat on one of the pegs by the door, which she opened. "Come on now, put your coat on and get going. That sweet man needs you. Just let me know if I should take the children home with me."

Clara considered the eggs, her coat beside Alison's, and Alison herself. She also considered everything Jonah had done for her. *Yes,* she thought, *making sure he's all right is the Christian thing to do, and I owe him at least that much.*

The frost in the yard crunched beneath her shoes. Only a few red leaves clung to the maple. Hanging to the skeletal limbs, they resembled dying butterflies, red and withering in the still morning air. Clara's throat and sinuses burned with it. Her breath jetted from her nostrils. In the truck, she decided against the heat because of the short drive.

As she approached Jonah's mailbox, so did another vehicle. Clara pulled into the driveway. Behind her, the other vehicle did also. To her surprise, Tess climbed out and rushed to Clara's door to open it. "Are you here for the same reason I am?"

Clara faced the auburn-haired woman. Her cheeks were red, either from anger or cold—or from fear and concern? "How do I know what your reason is when you haven't told me?"

"Jonah won't answer his phone. He hasn't come to any guitar lesson for a while either, and I was going to check on him."

Tempted to slam the truck door in Tess's face, Clara grabbed the armrest. "That's what I was going to do."

"Good, because you should." Tess tilted her head to one side. Sunlight reflected off her glossy hair, exposing a few faint freckles dotting her cheeks and nose. "What's going on between you two? He used to talk about you and the children but he doesn't anymore." Straightening her head, she shook it and turned away. A minute passed, maybe more. When she turned back around, her green eyes glistened with tears. "I get it now. He's in love with someone he can't have like I am."

Clara assumed she meant Lydia for him and

Denver for her. "Well, things don't always work out, do they? That's what you get for interfering in your sister's marriage."

The green eyes widened. "For a Mennonite, you're one of the most judgmental people I've ever met. Things like love aren't so cut and dried in the real world."

"Love's an emotion. It takes strength and vows to God to control them. If you had practiced that instead of letting your emotions run wild, you wouldn't be in the situation you're in now."

The green eyes returned to their normal width. "I'll give you that. If I had time I'd tell you why, I would. What's important is Jonah. What's more important is whether you want him or not, because of you don't, I do." Tess raised her hand toward Clara's face, the thumb and index finger an inch apart. "I'm this far from falling in love with him." She lowered the hand. "But I can't because you broke his heart somehow. That poor man is in love with you and you can't even see it."

Heat flared in Clara's cheeks. "English lies," she spat. "We're just neighbors."

"You say that because you're afraid," Tess said, her voice softening. "I wasn't afraid when I fell in love with Denver, but I should've been. I knew he would never stop loving Eliza and I jumped in head first anyway. I was young and stupid and you're not. The rule against Amish and Mennonites marrying outside of the church is one of the strictest there is. I don't know how you can get by it, but with God, all things are possible. But," she added, her voice hard again, "if you refuse to tell him you love him, I'll be glad to take your place. He's single and so am I. I'll make sure he gets over you in time. I never had a chance with Denver, but I *do* have a chance with Jonah." She went to her open car door and faced Clara. "It's your choice. Either you go to him or I will."

Indecision almost brought Clara to her knees. Despite the repercussions of being Beachy Amish Mennonite, for longer than she could remember, she had wanted to believe Jonah loved her. If he did, how could they be together without her breaking her vows to God and the church?

Clara, sweetheart, like I always told you, with God, all things are possible.

In the still morning air, in a blur of emerald-green wings, a hummingbird hovered before Clara's face as if studying her.

Do you hear me, Clara? Love isn't just an emotion. Like with our love, it's the truest gift God gives us. You better run to it if you have the chance.

The hummingbird—an impossible site in

November—whirred away toward Jonah's house, fading away to a speck, then to a pinpoint, then to a question mark hanging within the recesses of Clara's mind.

She blinked. Tess was backing out of the driveway. Regret gripped Clara, even to the point of revelation. She had judged Tess so harshly when she had no right to judge anyone at all. *Abram is right about love*, she thought, *and now I need to follow my own love no matter what happens.*

She sped to the two-story house, slammed on brakes, and hurried to the front door to try the knob, which refused to turn. Hopping off the porch, she landed behind the shrubbery. At the living room window, she raised on tiptoe to peep in. Wearing his usual blue jeans, a gray work shirt, and white socks without shoes, Jonah lay on the sofa, eyes closed. In a white cloud, his breath hovered over his open mouth. At his collar, several buttons were undone, revealing chest hair. Clara rapped her knuckles against the glass. "Wake up, Jonah! I need to talk to you!"

He rolled away from her to face the back of the sofa.

Clara ran to the back of the house, her blue dress fluttering around her legs, and tried that door, which was also locked. At one of the windows beneath the porch, she studied the old-fashioned latch. Jonah had said he wanted to install modern insulated windows but had never gotten around to it. Still wearing her coat, Clara bashed her elbow into the glass until it shattered. The latch, coated with layers of white paint, refused to open. Gritting her teeth, she pinched and twisted the icy metal until it rewarded her by squeaking open. Next, she managed to shove the sash upward despite the coats of paint and climbed inside, falling into the floor in a heap and cracking her knees in the process. Like Jonah's breath, hers gathered around her face. She went to the thermostat in the hall and raised it, then hurried to the living room. *Idiot*, she told herself. *You need to close that window and cover it somehow, or it'll stay freezing in here.*

From her time in this kitchen before, when she and the children stayed here, she located a plastic trash can bag in the cabinet beneath the sink, found a roll of duct tape in a drawer, and secured the bag over the broken window.

At Jonah's side, she knelt on the hardwood floor, wincing at the pain in her knees, and shook his shoulders. "Jonah, wake up, it's Clara." She stood to get a better look at his face. Dark whiskers, possibly two weeks-worth, covered his face from cheeks to throat. White as the proverbial ghost, he moaned and tried to push her away, but he was too weak to do so. His hip bones pressed up from beneath the jeans. His cheeks were hollow and sunken. A thin film of phlegm whitened his lips. Only he knew when he had eaten and drank last, possibly for the same amount of time it took to grow those whiskers.

Thankful for the heat warming the room, Clara hurried to the kitchen. Before she opened the refrigerator or pantry, she took her phone out and called Alison. "You better take the children home with you. Jonah is weak from not eating or drinking. I'll stay with him until I know he can take care of himself."

"Of course you will," Alison said, with what sounded like humor in her voice. "Just call when you two get things straightened out." She paused. "Clara, I know I've teased you about Jonah, and I don't know how you can marry an English man, but other than Abram, Jonah will make a wonderful husband to you and a father to John and Edna. I'll be praying for you both. I love you."

Tears filled Clara's eyes. Her best friend was truly her best friend. All this time she had known what both Clara and Jonah needed in life to be happy—even in God's eyes—and it was each other.

In minutes, a can of vegetable soup steamed in a

bowl in the microwave. At Jonah's side once more, she raised the spoon to his lips. "You need to eat, Jonah. I need you strong again so we can talk."

Chapter 15

As Jonah's vision had done the last few days, it hazed in and out, in and out. Focusing on anything was impossible, much less identifying the shifting forms hovering over and around him. For all he knew, those forms were the ghosts of his guilt come to taunt him. Some wore hair of flames. Some wore hair of shadow. Some laughed. Some held him. Some gazed into his eyes with love, some with contempt. How dare he think he could love Clara and not suffer the consequences. All his life he had tried to do the right thing, to be a good person, to help others when he could. Hadn't he gotten Lydia away from her abusive father? Hadn't he comforted Tess with a hug the last time they were together, the same as she had done for him? Hadn't he helped Clara ever since Abram had died?

The metallic gleam of a spoon came toward his mouth. Time and time again he pushed it away. Time and time again it returned, until he couldn't even raise his hands.

Warm and somewhat salty, what could only be soup drizzled between his lips and down his throat, while a voice soothed him as if he were a child: "There you go, sweetheart. You've got to finish it, though. Then I'll let you rest."

What ghost would call him sweetheart? None that he knew of. Lydia had left him, gone to court Noah. How in the world had that come about? Instead of her dark hair, this ghost was one of those with hair of flames. *Tess,* he thought, *I could've loved you so easily. I'm sorry I couldn't. I'm not good enough, not kind enough, not worthy of anything, not even love. Regardless of your regrets about Denver, you're one of the most loving people I've ever known. You accept people for who they are, and that's why Eliza and Denver and your family have accepted you.*

With the soup reviving him somewhat, he raised a hand to the smooth cheek hovering nearby. "Who are you, ghost?"

The ghost removed a blue hair covering of some kind. Spirit fingers plucked at its flamed hair until it flowed down its shoulders and to its waist. Then it took Jonah's hands and clasped them within its hands. "I'm someone who loves you, Jonah. Don't you know that by now?"

He caressed the cheek, pale skin as soft as John and Edna's cheeks. Emotion filled his throat. "I don't know anything, ghost, except I've prayed and prayed, and God hasn't answered me."

The ghost raised Jonah's hands toward the pale face. Warm lips kissed his knuckles. "He's answered you, sweetheart. You just don't know it yet." The ghost left and returned with a glass. "Here," it said, lifting Jonah's head. "You're probably dehydrated."

He tasted water. Sweet and cool, like the rivers feeding the lake he loved so well, it revived him enough to realize how tired he was. "I need to sleep, ghost."

"Not until you empty this glass. If you don't, I'll never carry your big self to my pickup for a trip to the hospital. Come on now, drink."

Jonah did so, then closed his eyes. Who was this flame-haired ghost, come to haunt him with kindness? Letting the question drift away from his mind, he dozed off and on throughout the day, evidenced by the brightening light beyond his closed eyelids, followed by shadows lengthening across the room. Again and again the ghost returned. Again and again it lifted his head and raised the glass to his lips. Again and again it kissed his brow and murmured whispers of love and caring.

A day passed, maybe more, again evidenced by the brightening of the light and the lengthening of the shadows. The ghost unbuttoned his shirt and opened it to expose his chest. A cloth, warm and wet, scrubbed his skin. The ghost raised his arms. "Mmm, you stink. Let me get under here too." A giggle followed. "If you don't get off this sofa soon, I'll have to wash you like a newborn baby with a dirty diaper."

Jonah managed a chuckle. "I'd die of embarrassment, ghost."

The ghost dried him off with a towel. "I'll be back with your soup. You really should be getting better by now. Can't you open your eyes and look at me?"

Through slitted eyes, Jonah studied the ghost. So beautiful. So amazing. So … *"Clara?"*

The ghost—no, Clara—beamed the most brilliant smile he'd ever seen his life. "It's about time you came around." She fingered the button of his jeans." The last thing I want is to take your pants off to bathe you." She lowered her head, her cheeks reddening with embarrassment. "Until we're married, that is."

Sitting up, he shoved her hand away. "How long have you been here?"

"A day and a half—long enough to know you haven't been eating or drinking." She rose from her knees to sit on the coffee table. "I know you've been through a lot because of me. Please forgive me. I've been denying everything about us for so long— No, I've been *trying* to deny everything about us for so long, I didn't know which way was up and which was down. I'm done with that now. I love you, Jonah. Don't you love me too?"

Jonah leaned over to set his elbows on his knees. "Why are you here? You said you didn't want to see me again."

"Alison told me everything you did for Lydia and why. I can't imagine a father beating his loved ones."

"Then you know I asked her to marry me."

"And she turned you down to court Noah."

Jonah sat up straight. "I never saw that coming. That's how stupid I am."

Clara moved to the sofa and took one of his hands into both of hers. "You're not stupid at all. I know how it feels to lose someone I love, and I made you feel like that when I told you I never wanted to see you again. I'm sure you asked Lydia to marry you because of the pain you were in.

When I first started caring for you, I might've thought the same thing, but I never considered it. Now I know it's not that at all. Now I know I love you and want to marry you. I don't know how we'll make it work with you being English and me being Beachy Amish Mennonite, but I don't care."

Jonah put her hands in her lap. "You'll break your vows to God and to the church. I can't let you do that. Just taking care of me alone isn't proper. What will your community think?"

Clara turned on the sofa to fully face him. "I care what they think, but I care more about what God thinks. He brought us together, Jonah. We're not school children or teenagers with a crush. We're adults with an abiding love for each other that we'll share for the rest of our lives. It was a miracle when I found that with Abram. Now it's a miracle again since I've found it with you. I take my vows to God and to the church seriously, but I take our love as seriously as God would have me take it. With God, all things are possible, and that includes us." She took his hand again, kissed his knuckles, placed the palm to her cheek. "Don't you love me? Please say you do. I can't go through losing someone I love this much again. I'll survive for John and Edna, but that's all my life will be—survival. I'll still worship God, but I doubt I'll ever attend church again. I couldn't stand to see happy couples when I have no chance at happiness." Head down, she sobbed once. Hot tears wet Jonah's hand on her cheek.

Did he love her? He had been attracted to her, even admitting it once. Then he had fought those feelings—or had he? No, not really, and he hadn't fought the feelings growing beyond attraction either. Her choosing to court Vernon had pierced his heart like a fishhook can pierce a fingertip. In Pennsylvania, the night they took a ride in his truck, when he held her like a child who needed to be comforted, he thought he might love her then, but the impossibility of a relationship made him banish the thought. Then Vernon left, and hope bloomed until Noah moved here. Now she was free to love, but at what price? There was only one way to find out, God willing.

He tried to raise her face to his, but she refused, afraid at what he was going to say. "Clara, look at me."

She shook her head. "Don't. I'll die if you don't love me. Please ... please don't."

He placed his other palm to her cheek and gently forced her face up. "Love doesn't describe what I feel for you. When Abram died, I couldn't imagine how you felt." Jonah paused to swallow the emotion filling his throat. "But I could imagine how

I'd feel if I lost the one person I loved like you loved him. I saw you both on the farm, how you walked hand in hand, how you looked at each other, how he would sometimes carry John and Edna in his arms, how you'd slip your hand around his waist. I wanted that so bad that my heart ached with it. Now I'm standing on the edge of a cliff, one foot over it. I don't know how we can be together without one of us doing something to compromise our ideals."

Clara placed his hands on his, leaned closer, closer still. "But you do love me. Please say it. It's all I've dreamed about since you held me that night in your truck in Pennsylvania, maybe even before then."

Leaning back on the sofa, Jonah gathered her into his arms. "Remember when we met, when I offered you and the children a ride home when you were walking on the road?" Clara nodded. "I thought you were the funniest thing," he continued, "glaring up at me with your big green eyes and shaking your little head with your little pointed chin like an elf's. I started to ask if your ears were pointed like an elf's too, but I thought you might punch me in the nose with one of your clenched fists. For a Beachy Amish woman, you looked a sight, all red haired and red cheeked.

When I saw you and the children looking over your garden, I knew I had to help you with it. Then I spoke with John and Edna for the first time, and my heart broke for them not having a father." He entwined his fingers into hers and raised her hand to his lips to kiss it. "Yes, I love you, but I don't know what to do about it."

Clara snuggled into him, holding him tight. "We have time to talk about it. Alison came by—that's how I know everything. She's asked me if something were going on between us a few times. I guess she could tell somehow. She got me to check on you and took John and Edna home with her." Clara paused to look up at him. "Tess was about to check on you too. I met her at the end of your driveway. I was wrong to judge her and her relationship with Denver. She's so lonely, Jonah, it's … she reminds me of how I felt when Abram died. She made me see how I was afraid to love you. She said if I didn't want you, she did."

Jonah kissed her hand again. "She's an amazing woman and mother. Along with her family, I'll always value her and Denver and Eliza as some of the finest people I've ever met. I look forward to you getting to know them better. She can sing like no one I've ever heard."

Still weak from his days without food and water,

he worked his way up from the sofa. "I need a shower. Then we can head to Clarksville for something to eat. While we're there, we can figure out what to tell Samuel and everyone in your community about us."

Jonah showered, shaved, and dressed in clean clothes. Feeling human again, he met Clara at her house, where she had done the same, along with pinning her hair up and donning a kapp. Gratitude filled him, both for her and for how God had led her to him. She was a miracle in every way possible, and in no way did he intend to give her up because of the Beachy Amish Mennonite rule against a person marrying outside of the church.

During the drive to Clarksville, after he mentioned his baptism at Tess's church, Clara raised a subject he was expecting: why couldn't he join her Beachy Amish Mennonite community? If so, the question of them marrying would be answered.

He glanced at her. "I'm sure you know some of the things Amish and Mennonites don't allow. If you think about that, you might think about one of the things I disagree with."

Her mouth formed an O. "I hadn't thought of that. I understand how important it is to you."

"Can you think of another reason? If you can't, a

hint is Lydia."

"I already thought of that, and I completely agree." Clara tapped a fingertip to her chin. "Abram and I moved here a few months after the community started. Vernon wanted a community that was more open to new ideas." Clara looked away and back. "I need to tell you why he left. I think it has something to do with why he wanted new ideas."

Jonah listened intently. When Clara finished, his opinion of Noah grew to another level for helping her, while his understanding for Vernon's problem confirmed his desire for new ideas in his community. He told Clara he agreed, but he didn't know how to solve those issues. From his online research about the Beachy Amish Mennonites, they were firm in their Ordnung, something Jonah admired. Still, some things needed to change, and the only way to do that was to speak to Clara's community about it.

In Clarksville, he suggested they share a fried chicken salad at The Bridgewater, where they had eaten with Tess, Denver, and Eliza that time. After the waitress took their orders and brought iced tea with lemon, Jonah faced Clara. "Do you have any ideas? They'll have to be great."

Sipping tea, Clara lowered the glass. "Great

enough for Samuel and everyone to agree to let us marry might be impossible. You know we vote on things, but I doubt anyone would support breaking the rule against marrying outside of our community." Clara paused for more tea. "Alison might. I don't know."

Jonah drank tea also. "It's a mess. I don't want you or them to compromise your vows."

"Vows are one thing, compromise is another. The best solution is for you to join our church. As strongly as you feel about not joining, I don't know how to get everyone to compromise."

Leaning back in the booth, Jonah considered the two issues that kept him from becoming Beachy Amish Mennonite. With the right persuasion, the community might agree to one. The other one, though, would take nothing less than a serious conversation from the heart. Considering how that subject was affecting Amish and Mennonite communities, it was past time for that conversation to occur.

As they enjoyed the salad, he and Clara further discussed their problem, eventually arriving at a solution they hoped would work. Radical as it was, it might, but like he had already thought, it would take a serious conversation from the heart, and the sooner the better, like at the church service at

Alison's home next Sunday.

Chapter 16

Sitting on the bench at Alison's kitchen table beside Clara, Jonah tried not to fidget. After their meal in Clarksville last Saturday, they called Alison to ask Samuel if they could speak this morning. Clara asked Alison to not say about what, only that it was important. Alison agreed, adding how she hoped things would work out, plus, since she expected the conversation after the service to be extremely serious, she would have all the children take their lunches to the barn to eat.

She asked if the discussion should occur before or after the adults ate lunch. Jonah opted for before, hoping the discussion would end on a note where everyone could enjoy each other's company, possibly carrying the group discussion over to private ones to put to rest any fears about what he and Clara were going to propose. He was glad his nerves were on edge. If not, all the aromas of the food before him, the roast beef and chicken casserole, green beans and buttered potatoes, fresh-baked rolls and cakes, including his favorite—a pecan pie—would've tempted him beyond endurance.

Samuel finished the closing prayer, adding how he hoped the community could grow to the point of building a church soon, as worshipping in church instead of a home was the usual Beachy Amish Mennonite way. *Amazing Grace* followed. Although a voice or two sang off key, Jonah valued the words. To him, anyone could sing regardless of their voice. The purpose was to praise the Lord with the best a person could offer, including a heart filled with gratitude.

As the notes of the song faded, Samuel faced the congregation. "Alison received a phone call last week from Clara and Jonah. As you know, Jonah's been coming to church here off and on. He also, praise God, told me he was baptized within the past year at a church outside of Clarksville, where Tess Gray and her family attend. I have no idea what he and Clara wish to talk about, but they said it's important. We also agreed to let the children go ahead and eat in the barn, because this will be an adult conversation. I've put a table and chairs in there, and I already have a propane heater mounted on the wall for when I work out there in the winter."

Clara and the ladies filled plates for the children and took them to the barn. She had told John and Edna about the talk, so they didn't ask questions. When Clara and the ladies returned, Samuel stepped away from the simple wooden podium he had crafted from oak. "As the English say, Jonah, you're on."

At the podium, Jonah smiled at everyone, ending with Samuel. "Thank you for that, Samuel. Like the Bible says, laughter is like a medicine." Clearing his throat, he faced the congregation again, taking his time to make eye contact with each person. "First, thank you for welcoming me to worship with you. I've always felt at home amongst you, and although I haven't been here lately, it's because I've been dealing with some personal issues."

He paused to gather his thoughts. How would they react to his request? It wasn't unheard of, so they would likely welcome it. Doing so, though, depended on his proposals to follow. "I'm sure everyone is hungry, so I'll start by stating my first request. I humbly ask if I might join your community."

Eyes darted. Voices murmured. Samuel nodded. Taking the lack of frowns as a positive sign, Jonah continued. "I realize this might not be a surprise because I've been coming here, and you know Clara and I are good friends, but I can't consider joining without some clarity on two issues that trouble me. One is how Beachy Amish Mennonites don't allow musical instruments to accompany singing when the Bible says to worship God with musical instruments in Psalms ninety-eight, verses five and six."

Standing to the side with Alison, Samuel raised his hand. "It's to avoid pride in the person playing the instrument, Jonah. He or she would stand out from the rest of us. The community is stronger when we stand together instead of apart."

"I respect and understand that," Jonah said, meaning it. "Let me ask everyone this," he added, studying each face. "Is it pride to be grateful for the abilities God gives us?"

"I don't see how it could be since our abilities come from God," Alison said.

Samuel cut his eyes at her. "You're not setting an example of submission, Alison."

She crossed her arms. "You know very well we discuss all our family decisions, so I'm taking part in this one. Like the English say, 'a happy wife, a happy life.' You'd do well to remember that after this discussion. I can always add cayenne pepper to *your* serving of roast beef."

Jonah took the opening. "Y'all know I play the guitar. I take no pride in that ability. What I take is gratitude for God *giving* me that ability. Let's look at it another way—you might've heard the saying, 'Beauty is in the eye of the beholder.' Consider this—pride is in the eye of the person who assumes someone is prideful. I could assume Alison is prideful because of her delicious roast beef. I could assume Clara is prideful because of her red hair. I could assume anyone is prideful about anything, but without knowing the person's heart, I would be assuming. In my opinion, assuming something about someone is prideful in itself. Does anyone agree?"

"I do," Clara said. "I've judged others wrongly because of pride, and I'm ashamed of it."

From their talk yesterday, Jonah knew Clara meant Tess. He faced the others. "Who here hasn't judged by assumption? I know I have."

Alison raised her hand. "I have. I thought you and Lydia were living in sin. It wasn't my place to assume."

Jonah nodded. "Please, Alison, don't give it

another thought. Human weakness is difficult to overcome. All we can do is recognize our mistakes and try to do better." He faced everyone again. "Does anyone have any concerns about using a musical instrument in church? Like I said, it's about gratitude for the gift, not pride in the person playing. In fact, an instrument can raise worship to another level. You can feel it in your heart and soul. When that happens, you know music is a gift from God."

"If no one has any objections," Samuel said, "did you bring your guitar? I'd like to see what you mean."

Jonah went to Samuel and patted his shoulder. "It's all been taken care of. All I ask is for everyone to close their eyes while they listen. If it has the effect I think it will, it'll be a day to remember. I'll be right back."

Clara had hoped her community would allow Jonah to play, and it was about to happen. The talk had gone well so far. Now it was up to his gift of musical ability, sent down from Heaven by God like He sent His gifts to everyone.

The door opened again, evidenced by a rush of cold air on the back of Clara's neck. Footsteps passed and continued toward the podium. The metallic click of what must be Jonah opening his guitar case followed. Next came several strange, twanging sounds, and Jonah said the guitar needed tuning. Then came a full, resonate strum that echoed around the large room. A voice, clear and feminine, sang the first words to *Amazing Grace*. *No one here sings like an angel,* Clara thought. *Who can that be?*

Jonah's voice, deep and rich, joined the angel's voice.

That's Tess! I think she's playing the guitar and Jonah's singing with her. He didn't tell me this part of his plan, that rascal.

As the thrumming guitar continued to echo, Tess and Jonah's voices blended in perfect harmony, and Clara couldn't help joining in. From around the room, more voices transformed the song into pure sunlight. *This is why the Bible says to worship with musical instruments,* Clara thought. *No wonder Jonah wants to be able to play his guitar in church.*

The strumming ended. The singing faded. Jonah asked everyone to open their eyes. Wearing a knee-length green skirt and a white sweater, auburn hair in a ponytail, the guitar still strapped around her shoulders, Tess beamed a lovely smile and gave a little wave. "Hey, y'all, you sound great. Isn't God good?"

Standing beside Alison at the end of the table,

Samuel chuckled. "He certainly is, Tess. You made us sound amazing."

"No, sir. God's gift of music made everyone sound amazing. To me, a musical instrument helps with harmony, and harmony helps everything in our lives. We see things clearer, if you know what I mean. For myself, it helped me recognize some mistakes I made when I was younger. Like with music and Jonah's friendship, I'm blessed beyond anything I deserve, and that includes my family. They accepted me regardless of my mistakes, and it means the world to me." Tess cased the guitar and stood by Jonah.

"I couldn't have said it better myself," Samuel said, returning to the podium. Pausing, he faced everyone. "When we formed this community, we did so because we wanted a fresh start. Since, like Jonah said, Psalms ninety-eight says to worship with musical instruments, I don't understand the reason for not using them, or at least the simpler ones. I've heard electric guitars and drums on TVs in stores, and I don't think we need that." He paused again, looking around the room. "Do we need to vote on this, or does anyone have a concern about it?"

In the rocking chair in a corner, the elderly Mrs. Yoder raised her hand. "While we're voting, can we vote on us women folk wearing shorts and T-shirts in the summer? Some communities allow them as long as they cover the knee and don't show off our figures." She smiled. "Not that I have one to show off."

"I'd like that too," Alison said. "It's hot working outside in the summer."

Samuel frowned at her. "I don't know how I'd feel about other men seeing your legs. It's not proper."

Alison placed her hands on her hips. "Proper? If it's not proper, the problem is those men, not me. I can't control what men think. If they think improper thoughts, they should get down on their knees and beg God to cleanse their minds." She gestured toward Tess. "Look how beautiful Tess is dressed. Since all you fine men here have taken your vows to the church, I'm sure none of you have noticed, right, Samuel?"

Jonah held in a laugh. No doubt Alison meant none of the men had noticed Tess's legs, when even Samuel's gaze had lowered for a second when he had spoken to her at first.

Samuel's cheeks reddened. "Um, well ... she's not wearing shorts, Alison, so I don't see your point."

Sputtering laughter came from all the ladies, and

Clara stood. "I wouldn't mind shorts while I'm working in the heat. It's much more humid in Virginia than in Pennsylvania."

Samuel's cheeks paled. "I suppose it's all right if no one has an objection. Please raise your hands to pass the motion to allow the ladies to wear shorts and T-shirts. The shorts must cover the knee, and both the shorts and T-shirts must be loose fitting."

Every hand raised. Despite Samuel's stern expression, he raised his too. "All right then. From this point forward, we will allow simple musical instruments to accompany our singing and allow the ladies to wear shorts and T-shirts in summer." He faced Jonah. "You said you had two concerns before you would join us. What's the second one?"

Clara faced Jonah. "You surprised me with Tess. Now it's my turn." She went to the door and opened it. What sounded like three car doors closed. Seconds later, in came Vernon, Noah, and Lydia. Clara led them to the front and faced the congregation. "I'm sure everyone is wondering what Jonah's second concern is. I thought Lydia and Vernon could better explain it because of their experience with it." She went to Jonah's side, and Vernon took the podium.

"Hello, everyone, it's good to see you." Murmurs of welcome answered. Having forgotten to remove his wide-brimmed black hat, Vernon set it on the podium. "I don't mind telling you I'm nervous, but when Clara called me, I knew I had to help her and Jonah make their case." Beneath his black Sunday jacket, his chest heaved with a huge breath. "This isn't easy for me to admit, but I lied about leaving here. In fact, much of my life has been a lie. I knew there were rumors about me being married. Unfortunately, those rumors were true. Even worse, I courted Clara before my wife died. Shortly after we were married, she became mentally ill. The doctors tried everything, but nothing helped. Her parents understood how hard it would be for me to have a life if I did nothing but stay with her all the time, so they took her in. For years I've moved around to keep the rumor a secret, but Noah discovered it and told Clara. That's why our courtship ended. I can't put into words how sorry I am for what I did, and I hope you'll forgive me."

"You say your wife died?" Samuel asked.

Vernon nodded. "Right before I took that trip last year. It was to attend to her funeral."

"Then you could've married Clara if she forgave you. Did you ask her?"

"I considered my life of sin unforgiveable, but she forgave me during our phone call when she asked me to speak here today. The point is, Amish and Mennonites don't allow divorce—not even for situations where a spouse has absolutely no control over the issue."

"I don't understand," Samuel said. "No one here wants a divorce."

Vernon stepped aside, and Lydia took the podium. "That's why I'm here. Like with Vernon's rumor of having a wife, I'm sure some of you thought Jonah and I weren't related and were living in sin. We let people think we were brother and sister to avoid that, but it happened anyway. We understand being human and assuming the worst, and it's a special person who never assumes anything about someone, let alone the worst. Jonah's second concern about joining your community has to do with me." Lydia raised her crooked elbow and touched the scar. "My Mennonite father did this to me. He beat me and my mother, and I've been trying to get her to leave him because he wouldn't stop. When she and I told our bishop about it, he assumed we weren't being submissive. We felt betrayed, not only by him, but by my father. I knew Jonah because he lived near us. He saw me walking on the side of the road after my father broke my arm. I was in a stupor. All I knew was I needed to get away from my father before he killed me. Jonah took me to the hospital and I had surgery. I'll always have this scar to remind me of that. Mom lives in Harrisburg now. The bishop got my dad to repent. The first night she went back to him, he beat her again. Along with Vernon's example of how divorce should be allowed in a community, we have my mom's example, and that's Jonah's second concern." Lydia left to join Noah. He gave her a gentle smile and went to the podium. "Y'all —" He laughed. "Listen to me, sounding like a Virginian. "Clara and I were courting and it didn't work out, but Lydia and I are courting now. To say my heart is full would be an understatement. She and her mother said they would be willing to forgive her father if he would stop the beating. To me, that shows how big their hearts are … how big Lydia's heart is … and I couldn't love her more if I tried." He stepped aside. "Jonah, I'm sure you can better explain your concern than I can."

Jonah took the podium. The congregation's eyes focused on his. "If you're as hungry as I am," he said, "I'm sorry this is taking so long. I hope it'll only take a few more minutes. My concern is with men who abuse their wives or their family or both. Too many times it's hidden in Amish and Mennonite communities. Worse, too many times the victims are blamed."

He paused to look around the room. In the corner, Mrs. Yoder met his gaze. To her left—Jonah couldn't remember their names—a couple's stony faces verified the seriousness of the subject. The rest of the small community's members faced him as well, equal concern etched on their faces. Clara, however, mouthed, *I'm so proud of you,* which melted his heart. Sharing a slight smile with her, he faced everyone again. "Since I met Lydia—more-so since I met Abram and then Clara—I've done a lot of research into the Amish and Mennonites. I admire their commitment to God, to their families, and to their communities. I enjoy my work and love the outdoors, so I admire their work ethic and how they farm. The one thing I don't admire is how a man can abuse family members and get away with it."

Samuel raised his hand. "They don't get away with it, Jonah. They must repent and ask forgiveness."

"What happens if they do that and don't stop their behavior?" Jonah asked, trying to keep anger out of his voice. "You just heard what happened to Lydia."

Mrs. Yoder stood again. "I'm an old woman. I've seen my share of life and its troubles. Repentance and forgiveness is who we are as a community."

Jonah expected the older members of this community—Mrs. Yoder being the only one after her husband passed away last year—to guess what he was going to say and reject it. All he could do was wait and see what she would say.

"*But ...*" she continued, emphasizing the word, "I know something about this issue. A friend back home in Pennsylvania told me about an exhibit in Leola. It was of the clothes abuse victims wore when they were attacked." Mrs. Yoder's face contorted as if she were going to cry. "It's bad enough for grown women to suffer such a thing, but some of those dresses were worn by—" She fingered tears from her filling eyes. "Some of those dresses were worn by little girls only a few years old."

Around the room, all the women gasped and the men shook their heads.

She eased down into the rocking chair. "Jonah, I'm sure you have more to add. We can always heat our lunch in Alison's microwave."

Feeling the sting of tears himself, Jonah thanked Mrs. Yoder and went to the podium. He had seen that exhibit online, and it had broken his heart like it was now breaking hers. He faced everyone again. "Before I go on, let me say this—although abuse happens, in no way does it condemn all Amish and Mennonites. I'm not trying to do that and I hope everyone understands that. From some of the articles I've read online, more communities are taking a tougher stance against abuse, thank God. My question for this community is what kind of stance it will take if abuse happens here? More specifically, how will it handle it if the abuser repents but doesn't stop?"

A moment passed, then another. The couple Jonah couldn't name whispered to each other. Samuel crossed his arms, betraying his discomfort. Clara stared toward the floor, knowing their future hung in the balance of how her community—the community she loved and didn't want to leave— would meet such a serious challenge.

Vernon stepped to the podium. "Jonah, if I may."

All eyes focused on Vernon, including Jonah's. He harbored a small amount of ill will toward Vernon for lying to Clara, but the man had obviously taken his repentance to heart, or he wouldn't have admitted it so openly. He patted Jonah's shoulder. "For myself, I'd like to see this young man join this community. For myself, to answer this question, I'll return to the reason we came here. We wanted a fresh start. What that included at the time, we weren't sure. Like the explorers of old, maybe we were drawn to new lands, to new places, to new views like with the nearby lake. This is a chance for a fresh start. Amish and Mennonite communities are suffering because of abuse. For the most part, we're exactly what we strive to be—people who love God, family, and community." Vernon shook his head. "But to allow abuse in a community is to allow a cancer, especially if the abuser will not stop. We want our community to grow, to be a light to draw the faithful. The only way we can do that is to be honest about issues like these. Both Amish and Mennonites are leaving their communities. I don't know the exact number, but even one is too many. No doubt some leave for the temptation of the outside world, such as when Amish youth experience Rumspringa. No doubt as well, some leave because of their experiences with abuse. Should we give an abuser the chance at repentance to God? I say yes, but it should be up to the person who is abused if he or she accepts that repentance. I wouldn't dare make that choice for anyone, let alone someone who has been abused over and over again." Vernon stepped aside. "Jonah, unless I miss my guess, you have a final proposal to make. I hope it's accepted, because I'd dearly love to see you become a part of this community."

Thanking him, Jonah again went to the podium. "As far as a proposal, I—"

Alison left Samuel's side and went to the table. She took a large carving knife from the platter of roast beef and waved it in the air. "I know we aren't supposed to be violent, but I propose we tell any new members what I'll do to them with this knife if a single hair is harmed on the head of a loved one. I never heard of such a thing until today. Just the thought makes my blood boil." She jabbed the knife into the roast and returned to Samuel's side to cross her arms.

"I understand your anger," Jonah said to her. "I hope my proposals will stop anything like that from happening in the first place." Once more he faced the congregation. "My first proposal is to allow a family member to decide if they forgive abuse. For anyone to attempt to tell another person how to feel about it is wrong. Only that person knows how they feel, or if they can forgive. My second proposal concerns the person who accepts forgiveness but is still abused. If all else fails, that person should be allowed a divorce. I know this is a radical idea, but the Bible allows divorce in particular cases. I agree it shouldn't be recommended, but it should be allowed. Like with

Vernon, who has sincerely seen the error of his ways, a person should be allowed that chance. Otherwise, we would have a hypocrite and a liar in our community, and he or she would tear it down instead of building it up."

Jonah paused to see if anyone had anything to add. When no one did, he continued. "My last proposal is this—any person who refuses to repent their abuse, or repents and continues to abuse, must be turned over to law enforcement. If we tell new members this, I hope they will understand how seriously we take the safety of our congregation, and that will stop any abuse before it happens." Sensing the need for a little humor to ease the stony expressions around the room, Jonah faced Alison. "We can also add how sharp Alison keeps her carving knife, and what she'll do with it if the need arises."

Again, Mrs. Yoder worked herself up from the rocking chair. This time she shuffled to the podium and set her elbows on the oak surface. "I've always thought I'd make a good deacon." She smiled at Vernon, who wasn't smiling. "Don't look at me like that, Vernon, I know I can't be one. You men count on us women to keep you fed and clothed and your children the same. The church would fall apart without us, so there." She faced everyone. "For myself, I accept Jonah's proposal. Unless I miss my guess, though, he has an important reason for wanting to join us. What do you say, Clara? Am I right or not?"

Jonah waved Clara over. Red-cheeked, she joined him. "We can't get anything past you. Mrs. Yoder." She faced everyone. "Jonah and I want to marry."

Alison snorted laughter. "Tell us something we didn't know, Clara."

"Me too," Lydia said. "Ever since he plowed her garden, I knew the love bug had bitten him. Clara this, Clara that. John this, Edna that. That's all I heard."

"I should've seen it myself," Vernon said. "I knew they were close, but I didn't know they were *this* close."

"I suspected it," Noah said. "That's why I ended our courtship." He went to Jonah and shook his hand. "Congratulations." He faced Clara. "I hope you'll both be very happy."

Still at the podium, Mrs. Yoder gave it a sharp slap. "I hate to break up the party, but we need to vote on Jonah's proposals. Allowing divorce and bringing law enforcement into our community is serious business. When the word gets out, other bishops might have something to say about it."

"That's one of the things I like about the Beachy Amish Mennonites," Vernon said. "They tend to allow communities to decide how they handle these matters by voting. I've even read on a Beachy Amish website where a single family would move in order to start a new community."

Samuel went to Vernon. "It takes a big man with a big heart to admit his mistakes. If everyone agrees, I'd like to invite you back as bishop."

"I appreciate that, Samuel, but I still carry a lot of guilt about my mistakes." He motioned Jonah over. "Maybe this fine man would consider the job. Not only does he have a good head on his shoulders, he considers the safety of his flock of the utmost importance. What do you say, Jonah?"

Jonah's mouth fell open. "Well, I never thought about it."

Vernon laughed out loud. "Don't worry, I meant after the wedding instead of now. If you'll allow me, I'd like to try my hand at being a deacon, like in my younger days. That'll give you plenty of time with your bride. Of course, you'll have to be baptized into the Beachy Amish Mennonite church."

Marveling at the turn of events, Jonah faced everyone. "It looks like we've got a baptismal and a wedding to plan." He looked down into Clara's brilliant green eyes. "Well, Clara, do you have a date in mind?"

Beaming a smile up at him, she squeezed his hand. "Any time after lunch. I'm starving."

Chapter 17

Picking at a piece of pecan pie after lunch, Clara strolled around the room, stopping here and there as various conversations ebbed and flowed around her: Samuel asking Vernon to please return as a bishop and let him be a deacon to give him time to learn more of the Bible; Jonah asking the same because he should learn more of the Bible before considering the position of bishop, although he would certainly consider being a deacon; Lydia telling Noah how happy she was since they were marrying at the end of November; Noah saying they needed to find a place to live since Vernon was returning to the community and his home; Lydia's reaction of saying she would love to live here as long as her mother could live with them; Alison saying how nice it would be to spend time with

Lydia again; Samuel saying as long as they behave, that is; Mrs. Yoder saying to let them alone because a little innocent fun never hurt anyone; the couple whose name Jonah couldn't remember saying how wonderful it felt to be a part of this community; John and Edna asking Jonah over and over if he was really marrying their mama, and when could he please, please, please take them fishing again?

And then there was Tess.

As lovely as daybreak, she stood by herself in a corner, arms folded, blinking now and then, no smile. A sudden pang of pity filled Clara.

As amazing as Tess's relationship with Eliza, Denver, and her family was, she had lost Jonah like she had lost Denver, so she must be wondering if God would provide a man to cherish her like all the men here cherished their loved ones.

Clara threw the leftover pie away, set the plate by the sink, and joined Tess. "I hope you forgive me for thinking the worst of you and Denver. For you to give him up to Eliza when you didn't have to shows more courage than most people have."

Tess fingered a tear from the corner of one eye. "I had to do the right thing, Clara. I wouldn't have been able to live with myself if I hadn't." She touched Clara's arm. "You and Jonah—well ..." Withdrawing her hand, she cleared her throat.

"You give me hope of finding someone too. My children and family mean the world to me, but it's not the same. I'll always regret my choices when I was younger." She smiled. "I'll always regret not stealing Jonah from you too, but I'll never regret doing the right thing."

A sudden urge to do the right thing overwhelmed Clara. She placed her hands on Tess's shoulders and pulled her close for a hug. "I think we should be friends," she whispered in Tess's ear. "What do you think?"

Pulling away, Tess fingered more tears from her eyes. "I'd love that. I haven't had a friend outside of my family since we left Ohio." She gave her hands a little clap. "Oh! If you can, you and Jonah and your children should come to Thanksgiving dinner at Denver and Eliza's home. The Andrews and Gray families always get together for it. We'd love to have you."

Although Clara appreciated the invitation, other matters were more pressing. "What about next year? Jonah and I and the children need to travel to Pennsylvania and tell my parents about us. I wish we could get married in the fall, like Amish and Mennonites usually do, but he needs to study for his vows to the church. Planning a wedding takes a lot of time too."

Tess apologized for not thinking of that. "Next Thanksgiving will be good." She patted her tummy. "Maybe you and Jonah will have a bun in the oven by then."

Clara frowned. "Well, I usually make yeast rolls for Thanksgiving, but I could make buns."

Tess leaned close to Clara's ear. "I meant maybe you'll be expecting by then," she whispered. She stood upright again. "But yeast rolls sound great too."

Clara snorted laughter. "Tess, I think we're going to be best friends." She glanced at Lydia and Alison, their heads together as they talked about something. "I've always got room for another best friend."

Jonah came over. "What's all this whispering about, ladies?"

Tess grinned at Clara. "I was just asking Clara if I could kiss the groom before y'all get married. If I do, maybe I can steal you away from her yet."

Clara shrugged. "With all the time you two spent taking guitar lessons, I thought you had kissed already." She shoved Jonah toward Tess. "Go ahead. It'll be a good test."

Jonah hurried back to her side. "A test for what?"

Tess giggled. "I think he just passed, Clara."

"Darn right," Jonah said. He winked at Clara. "I won't deny thinking about it, though."

Tess patted his arm. "And now you'll never think about it again." She hugged him and then Clara. "Let me get back home. Jonah, if Clara *lets* you, you can still take guitar lessons. See y'all later."

As the door closed behind Tess, Clara faced Jonah. "I was just telling Tess how I wish we could get married this fall, but we have too much to do."

"I agree, like visiting your parents and planning the wedding. Do you mind a non-traditional wedding in the spring, after we plant our gardens?"

Clara poked his ribs. "Our *garden*, not gardens. You won't need one then."

"Oh, that's true. I was just talking to Noah and Lydia. They want to know if I'll sell them my house. I know you want to stay where Abram is, so I can move in with you."

Clara wondered if Jonah knew the saying Tess had told her about babies. "I don't know. We don't have enough room for the buns in my oven."

"Do *what?*" Jonah asked, his eyebrows rising. "Is that some Beachy Amish recipe I don't know about?"

"Tess told me. It means when I'm expecting."

Jonah scratched his head. "Oh. I've heard that, but not like you said it. Sure, we can add on however many rooms you'd like. I've always admired how Amish or Mennonite men help with construction projects."

Clara popped his arm. "It's too bad you didn't have that much help after you burned my house down."

Noah and Lydia came over. "I didn't hear what you said, Clara," Lydia said, "but I see you've got him trained already. I like it when the men have to submit to the women."

Jonah winked at Clara. "She was just telling me we need to add some rooms onto the house for our buns."

"'Buns?'" Noah asked, his nose scrunching up. "Is that a recipe for bread I don't know about?"

Covering a laugh, Lydia lowered her hand. "I'll explain it after we're married. It's a recipe you'll like, I promise."

They left to speak with Mrs. Yoder, who was sharing her favorite roast turkey and stuffing recipe with Alison. Saying it sounded interesting because he enjoyed cooking, Jonah joined them.

Sitting at the table with a piece of pecan pie each, Edna and John chatted about how they always knew Jonah and Mama would get married, plus how much they looked forward to him living with them.

Clara had expected them to say how much they looked forward to him taking them fishing. Instead, she took it as a blessing that they weren't thinking too much about fishing. After all, they understood the difference between trivial things, thanks to her and Abram teaching them God's word.

Marveling at those blessings, Clara left the steady murmur of happy voices for the porch. Bright sunlight provided a hint of warmth. A cool breeze provided a hint of winter. God's love provided both, along with the love welling up inside her for how He had blessed her when she thought she had lost everything by losing Abram.

She fingered the sleeve of her blue dress. Yes, she and Jonah had much to do before a wedding. For one, she needed to make her wedding dress. For two, he needed to study and take his vows to join the church. For three, they needed to add onto the house in preparation for the wedding. If as many people attended as she hoped, they would need as much room as possible. Then again, if they waited until spring, after they planted their garden, the warmth would allow an outdoor wedding, with the barn large enough for plenty of tables for plenty of food for plenty of guests.

In Clara's dress pocket, her cell phone vibrated. Recognizing Mama's number, she raised it to her ear. "Good morning, Mama. It's a beautiful day in Virginia, nice and warm. How cold is it up there in Pennsylvania?"

"Now, now, Clara. As you well know, Pennsylvania is a perfectly lovely state."

"It is, but I have a feeling you didn't call to tell me that."

"Not at all. What's this I hear about Noah courting some person named Lydia? She's not Jonah's sister is she, the woman who drove you up here the last time? I've been hoping you'd call to invite your father and I to a wedding, and I heard about this Lydia person from Noah's own parents."

Clara paused for a grin. "You can attend Noah's wedding. Maybe I'll see you there with my own sweetheart. Since you just mentioned Jonah, we're getting married in the spring."

"Your *driver*? I didn't hear you right. This phone must be broken. Please repeat what you said."

"Yes, he drove me there last year. He's my English neighbor. We're in love and we're getting married."

The clatter of plastic striking a hardwood floor came from Clara's phone, followed by her mother yelling for her father to take the phone. "Clara," he said, "what in the world is your mother talking about."

"I need to sit down," Mama moaned. "I can't believe my own ears."

Papa chuckled. "She's gone, honey. Now tell me what's going on. When it comes to your happiness, I trust you and shouldn't have given you a hard time about moving back home. You made the perfect choice in Abram, God rest his soul, so if what Noah's parents say is true, I'm sure you had a reason for deciding against him."

"I didn't decide against him, Papa. Noah's a dear friend, but that's not enough to marry him."

"Well, I wouldn't want you to marry someone you don't love. Why's your mother asking you about that fellow who drove you here last year? Jonah, right?"

Clara knew the story would take too long for the phone. "I'll just say this—he and I and the children are coming for Thanksgiving. We'll tell you everything then, all right?"

"I'd like a hint now, Clara. If not, your mother will worry me to death about it."

"Just tell her God has blessed me beyond belief and I'll see y'all on Thanksgiving."

Papa chuckled again. "I kind of like that word 'y'all.' All right then, we'll see you on

Thanksgiving. And Clara?"

"Yes?"

"Whatever you decide, I know you'll choose love. I also know you'll choose with John and Edna in mind, and that means a lot. We love you. See you soon."

Clara slipped the phone in her pocket. Another blessing: Papa learning to trust her. Mama did too, but the shock of thinking her daughter would leave the Beachy Amish Mennonites to marry an English man was too much to bear. Clara giggled. Maybe she shouldn't have teased her like that, but sometimes a son or daughter had to teach a parent a lesson.

Then again, sometimes parents need to open their minds to new things, such as realizing home is where the family is, not where a house is. Since that was the case, Clara prayed for God to provide even more blessings next spring.

Chapter 18

In front of her dresser mirror, Clara stood as still as possible. If not, Alison, Lydia, Tess, and Mama might complain as they pinned her hair, fussed over the blue dress, set the white kapp on her head, and fluttered around as if they were a flock of bluebirds warbling about the pretty lady about to get married.

"Oh, my," Mama exclaimed. "I love this shade of blue. It's exactly like the dress I wore when I got married." She touched the hair at her temples. "It's too bad my hair is turning gray, unlike yours, Clara."

"It's better to turn gray than to turn loose," Tess said, pinning the kapp into place. "Papa's is starting to get thin."

"I don't understand," Mama said. "Is that some

English saying you learned since you left the Amish and moved to Clarksville?"

Alison sputtered laughter. "It means it's better to have gray hair than to have no hair."

"That's right," Lydia said. "Tess said Absalom's hair is getting thin. That's what she meant."

"He certainly is a big bear of a man," Mama said.

"That's what Mama calls him," Tess said. She faced Clara. "Turn around and let's see how you look."

Clara did so, and the ladies oohed and ahed, saying how beautiful she was. "I think y'all are beautiful too," Clara said. "We all match."

"We're supposed to match," Tess said. "We're your bridesmaids." She touched the head covering she wore, similar to what unmarried Mennonite women wore: a small white cloth over her auburn hair in a bun.

"You're the only unmarried lady here," Alison said. "You need to do something about that."

"Well," Tess said, slapping her hands to her hips, "I keep losing my men. Isn't that right, Clara?"

Clara faced the mirror again. "We won't go there."

Mama went to the window. "There must be at least 150 people here." She paused. "Jonah certainly looks handsome in his black pants and white shirt and suspenders. He's quite the Beachy Amish Mennonite gentleman."

Lydia went to the window. "So's Vernon. Mama can't tear herself away from him."

Tucking a strand of hair beneath the kapp, Clara smiled. Unfortunately, that smile came with a mix of regret. Last year, Lydia's father, depressed because his family wasn't home at Christmas, had committed suicide. Lydia and her mother mourned the loss, saying they had prayed for him time and time again to overcome whatever had made him harm them.

To Clara and Jonah, it reiterated the fact that things needed to change, the ideal being to get medical or psychiatric help for any Amish or Mennonite person who exhibited such behavior.

Behind her, evidenced by Tess's reflection in the mirror, the lovely young woman went to the huge king-sized bed, patted the quilt, and looked around the room. "I love the additions to your house. Four rooms and two bathrooms, right?"

Lydia opened a door beside the dresser. "I like the master bath myself. That shower is big enough for two people."

Turning from the window, Mama frowned. "Why would two people shower at the same time?"

Grinning at Clara, Tess winked at Alison and Lydia and mouthed, *It's a good place to make buns.*

Mama checked her watch. "Clara, it's time."

"Can y'all give me a minute with Tess?"

Mama kissed her cheek. "Of course we can, sweetheart." She waved at the other ladies. "Come along now, let's give Clara a moment."

As the door closed, Tess went to Clara and took her shoulders in her hands. "Are you nervous?" she asked, questioning Clara's green eyes with her own.

Although Clara and Jonah and the children had spent Thanksgiving and Christmas with her parents, they had spent many Saturdays with both the Gray and Andrews families, even to the point of feeling as if she had gained two more families. They felt the same way, now within the crowd outside waiting for the wedding.

She wondered if Abram could see them all, could see John and Edna waiting with Tess's, Eliza's, and Alison's children, could see the sky, bright and blue and cloudless, could see the five tables in the barn filled with all kinds of food, desserts, and beverages, could see Jonah waiting near Vernon by the door of the barn, where, sadly, all of this had been set in motion.

Tess squeezed Clara's shoulders. "Are you all

right? I understand being nervous. Maybe I'll find out one day, you know?"

"I hope you do. I feel … I guess guilty is the best word. After everything you've been through, I hope you can find someone who deserves you."

Tess lowered her hands from Clara's shoulders. "Maybe I don't deserve anyone because I almost took Denver from Eliza."

"But you didn't."

"I wanted to. I told you much I loved him … love him still." Tess sat on the bed. "The feelings I was having for Jonah proved I can have them for someone besides Denver. I just have to be patient and see who God sends me."

Clara joined her, took one of her hands into both of hers. "Don't tell Alison, but I think you and I are closer than she and I are. We've lost our loves, and now we're trying to bounce back. I thank God every day for sending me Jonah."

Tess kissed Clara's cheek. "And I thank him for sending me you. Denver and I are close, but there are some things—feelings rather—I can't share with him. I can only do that with another woman, and that woman is you."

Clara knew what Tess meant. Even though she had Eliza, sometimes it seemed a woman outside of a family could only fill a place in the heart that only that woman could. She stood. "Can you give me a minute? Wait by the screen door and I'll be there soon."

When the door closed behind Tess, Clara sat on the bed and opened the nightstand drawer. Still wrapped in a handkerchief, the tiny quartz stone Jonah had given her on the shore of Buggs Island Lake beckoned. She unwrapped it and held it to the sunlight streaming through the window. Although the flaws shown as tiny dark lines, the brilliance of the stone revealed the light, just like God revealed the light in each and every person if they accepted Him into their hearts.

Clara had been blessed beyond measure. Now she would keep this stone until her death, to pass down to her family along with her and Abram and Jonah's stories, to remember to live, to love, and most important of all, to forgive.

With the stone safely in the drawer again, she met Tess at the screen door. "Hey, there, girlfriend. Let's get this wedding on the road."

Arm in arm, they stepped out onto the porch. Waiting with a camera at the bottom of the steps, Noah clicked a few shots. "It's about time you two. I bet everyone's getting hungry."

Clara and Tess hurried to the edge of the crowd. Women raised hands to their mouths as if to say,

Oh, isn't Clara beautiful. Nodding, men looked at each other as if to say, *yes, she certainly is.* Then they all looked skyward as if to say, *thank you, Lord, for all your many blessings. Amen.*

Papa offered his arm to Clara. "Hello, sweetheart. I know I've told you how much I like Jonah, but it bears saying again. He's a fine young man, and your mama and I couldn't be happier."

Nearby, Noah clicked more photos. Tess left Clara and went to Vernon, where she took her guitar from its stand and played and sang *How Great Thou Art.*

More voices joined hers, and by the end, several guests were wiping tears of gratitude for God's many blessings.

Beside Oneita, the big bear himself, Absalom, honked his nose in a handkerchief, likely remembering Eliza's wedding. Oneita patted his shoulder. Beside her, Eliza wiped tears. Beside Eliza, Denver gave Clara a thumbs up and mouthed, *You go, girl.* On the other side of the path through the crowd to Vernon, Clara's brother and sister and their spouses and their children grinned while looking at each other, happy to be gaining a fine brother-in-law and uncle. In front of them, Mama waited, wiping tears. Nearby stood Mrs. Yoder, who winked a gray eye at Clara while waving her forward.

The song ended, words and notes fading. Beside Jonah, Clara released Papa's arm and faced Vernon.

As she listened to the vows, something at the open doors of the hay loft above caught her eye. Any other time, the shock might've dropped her to her knees, but not this time.

Standing there in his dark pants and white shirt, suspenders over his shoulders, brown hair covered with a wide-brimmed straw hat, Abram waved and pointed down.

She looked at the dirt by her feet, exactly where Abram fell, exactly where his right hand clawed as his last breath left his broken body, exactly where she had run back to kneel and beg him not to go, not to leave John and Edna and her.

His hand …

His fingers weren't clawing in the dirt; only one finger was moving.

Drawing something?

Clara looked back up at the open loft doors.

No Abram. Nothing but the memory of how he had drawn a hummingbird in the dirt.

They loved watching them dart around the feeder she used to hang on the porch. He said if anything ever happened to him, he would send one as a sign that he was safe and sound in Heaven, and the one thing he wanted most of all for her was to find love again. Although tears filled Clara's eyes, joy filled her heart.

Abram had sent the hummingbird she had seen, not only once but twice. What a blessing he had been—and would always be—in her life, carried on in John and Edna's eyes and smiles.

Vernon's vows, which had transformed to a soft drone, became clear again. Along with the traditional vows, Clara and Jonah had written their own, inspired by the single poem she had written about love, and it was time to say them together.

"I have found in you, my love, my heart's fulfillment. I promise to always listen, to always cherish, and to always share our lives as one. Praise God for His blessings of love, for they will never fail us. Amen."

Vernon closed his Bible. "Let us pray. Dear Lord, thank you for Clara and Jonah. Be a light unto them through all the days of their lives. Shine upon them regardless of the task, regardless of the sorrow, regardless of their happiness. Surround them with family and friends. Allow our community to grow as it is doing now, with people who have heard how we will give the sinner a chance to repent, but also how we will keep our members safe. Thank you for our church being built down the road.

Thank you for providing the land nearby for us to come together as a community. Thank you for the schoolhouse across the road from the church, where Alison will teach in a few months. Our cups runneth over, Lord. And thank you for your Son, Jesus. Blessed is his name. Amen." Opening his eyes, he faced Clara and Jonah. "Through the power vested in me by our Lord, I now pronounce you husband and wife." He leaned close to them. "Like with a new garden, our community is breaking new ground with our changes. If you two would like to share a kiss, I have no objection."

Mrs. Yoder clapped her hands. "It's about time, Vernon. I've always thought it was silly for a couple to not kiss in one of our weddings."

Jonah took Clara's face in his hands. "Well, Mrs. Ellis?"

Clara stood on tiptoe and wrapped her arms around his neck. "Do you even have to ask, Mr. Ellis?"

As they kissed, everyone clapped. "All right!" Noah yelled. "Time to come up for air!"

Clara ended the kiss and faced the crowd. Although some cheeks were red with embarrassment, several couples smiled at each other with complete adoration, and several people were laughing with Noah.

Jonah waved his hand in the air. "Thank you all for coming, but I don't know who many of you are."

A Mennonite couple stepped forward. "We're the Johnsons, Mr. Ellis. We heard about the changes concerning the uh … well, it's too sensitive a subject to talk about here, but we're thinking about joining your community."

"That's makes four couples since Thanksgiving and eight families altogether," Vernon said.

"Please," Jonah said to the couple, "this isn't my community, it's God's community." He smiled at Clara. "Just like he brought Clara and I together, he brought this community together. We'd be glad to have you."

Clara faced Vernon. "Please bless our meal, Vernon."

He bowed his head. "Dear Lord, with hearts filled with gratitude, we humbly ask for your blessings on this food and on those who prepared it. May it nourish our bodies and give us strength for the days to come. Amen."

All around the yard, picnic tables Jonah had rented gradually filled with people. Forks and spoons raised. Either sweet tea with lemon or lemonade followed. Sitting with Clara and Jonah, Papa and Mama mentioned all the land nearby for sale, and Jonah chuckled. "Most of it is either mine or Clara's. If you're interested, we'll make you a good deal. Then I can afford to rent a pontoon boat to take John and Edna fishing more often."

"It is a beautiful lake," Mama said. She faced Papa. "We've spent most of our lives living near our other children and grandchildren. What if we moved here when you retire?"

"Not a bad idea." Papa grinned at Jonah and Clara. *"Y'all."*

Clara glanced at the open doors of the hay loft. Time had seemed to pass so quickly since that terrible day when Abram fell. Had it really been three years?

Done with her meal, she excused herself and left for the oak behind the house, where she ran her fingertips over the new coat of white paint on Abram's cross. Thought after thought careened through her mind: thoughts of mourning, courting, and finally, of choices.

God sends us here to do the best we can. If we follow His word to love Him, family, and friends as we love ourselves, earning our way through work, having gratitude for something as simple as waking in the morning, we can be blessed beyond measure.

Behind Clara, footsteps shuffled closer. A hand,

warm and familiar, slipped into hers. Jonah patted the cross with his other hand, then faced Clara. "I hope Abram knows I'm keeping my promise to look after you and John and Edna if something happened to him."

Clara slipped her arms around Jonah's waist and lay her head on his chest. Because of his concern for the victims of abuse, their community was growing. Because of her forgiveness to Vernon and friendship with Tess, her heart was filled near to bursting. Because of Abram's devotion to her and the children, God had blessed her with love when she had least expected it.

She gazed up into her husband's caring eyes.

"I'm sure he knows, sweetheart. I'm sure he knows."

ABOUT THE AUTHOR

J. Willis Sanders lives in southern Virginia, with his wife and several stringed musical instruments.

With fourteen novels completed and more on the way, he enjoys crafting intriguing characters with equally intriguing conflicts to overcome. He also loves the natural world and, more often than not, his stories include those settings. Most also utilize intense love relationships and layered themes.

His first idea for a novel is a ghostly World War II era historical that takes place mostly in the midwestern United States, which utilizes some little-known facts about German POW camps there at the time. It's the first of a three-book series, in which characters from the first continue their lives.

Although he loves history, he has written several contemporary novels as well, and some include interesting paranormal twists, both with and without religious themes.

He also loves the Outer Banks of North Carolina, and he has written three novels within different time frames based on the area, what he calls his Outer Banks of North Carolina Series. As of

January 2023, he's writing another novel about the area.

And yes, he enjoys learning about the variations of Amish culture, which inspired his Eliza Gray and Clara Engelman series.

Other hobbies include reading (of course), vegetable gardening, playing music with friends, and songwriting, some of which are in a few of his novels.

To follow his work, visit any of these websites:

https://jwillissanders.wixsite.com/writer

https://www.facebook.com/J-Willis-Sanders-874367072622901

https://www.amazon.com/J-Willis-Sanders/e/B092RZG6MC?ref_=dbs_p_ebk_r00_aba u_000000

Readers: to help those considering a purchase, please leave a review on Amazon.com, Goodreads.com, or wherever you bought this book. They help authors more than you may realize.